All Embracing and Other Stories
Dave Pescod

First published in 2012 by Route
PO Box 167, Pontefract, WF8 4WW
info@route-online.com
www.route-online.com

ISBN: 978-1-907862-07-6

Dave Pescod asserts his moral right to be
identified as the author of this book

Cover Image
Andrew Love

Cover Design
Dave Pescod

Printed by Lightning Source

A catalogue for this book is available from the British Library

Route is supported by Arts Council England

Contents

For my father

All Embracing

What you wear is important. You need to look smart and professional, but not too noticeable. I always use a pink lipstick, never red, and subtle make-up with my hair down, well brushed. You must look for a large group, the larger the better. Watch from a distance to see that there is some lack of organisation, and a relaxed approach to the order of events. More formal, organised parties will not work.

I often take a discreet photograph of the group at this early time, to keep in my album and look at on long winter nights. I've begun my second album, the photographs remind me of good practice, and the most memorable occasions.

I visited Heathrow several times, but people are tense there, preoccupied with purchasing duty frees and other distractions. I did try a funeral once but it felt awkward, dressed in black, and rather inappropriate for my intentions. I recommend railway stations: Waterloo, Kings Cross and especially Liverpool Street with the Stansted Express. Here, it's easy to see when the moment is right, as most of the groups will be going to the airport, and the times are well advertised on the noticeboards.

About ten minutes before departure, I make my move, joining as one of the latecomers, when they gather by the ticket barrier. The atmosphere will change as the moment becomes imminent, when shyer members position themselves at the back, and bolder or responsible ones take their places. The first will embrace more meaningfully, generally a leader of the hosts and an official from the visitors. Then others will follow quite quickly, gradually embracing all those around them, becoming more emotional and vulnerable, not wanting to be left out. This is the moment. You must move quickly, mingling in with the host group and smile as you approach the first embrace. Occasionally, you will need to say how wonderful it has been, and how much you will miss them, but you will hear the others, and it's best to follow their examples, sometimes using Christian names, to reassure them. Be quick, but enjoy the embrace before you pass on to the next person. I never kiss, as it is overfamiliar, and could jeopardise your position. They will be happy to embrace you, accepting that they do not recognise you, but presume that you are someone working behind the scenes. They will be as anxious as you, about their farewell and proper etiquette. Their generosity can be touching and moving. After a few embraces it is best to make an excuse and depart as quickly as you came, before they have time to confer about your identity.

It is easy to be seduced by the warmth of the embraces, but discipline is called for, to avoid overindulgence. In some early operations, my timing was wrong and I was pursued; once losing a Gucci shoe at Waterloo. I learnt self-control, and the need to withdraw early, knowing I can savour the moment at home, later.

When you hold someone; you hold a little bit of them forever. You hold their past and their future, and by the way they embrace you, they reveal their vulnerability and their strength. This makes me feel warm, part of something bigger.

For me, it is only natural to need some physical contact with other humans and this method has no complications. A woman in my position finds it reassuring, while I hope it brings some comfort to them. My London flat is well positioned for the stations, and even though I am getting older, I still set out once a week, to be embraced.

Rising Laughter

He's snoring again. It's worse since they changed his medication. I can't sleep and I can hear the neighbours talking in bed, through the wall. I can't hear the exact words, only the pattern. It undulates fast and slow, and ends with a pause when she laughs. It gets louder and he joins in. They'll wet themselves if they keep laughing like that. I get up and go to the kitchen and can't help smiling at the strange sound of their infectious laughter.

It's been ages since Roy left the flat to brave the world, and even longer since we had a laugh. He's lost somewhere in his body, helpless in a dark place, just like his dad. But I don't want to give up trying. Those bloody pills aren't the answer.

He took me dancing when I was sixteen, and I couldn't see any sign of it. He'd laugh like anyone else, chortle and shake, become possessed as good as anyone. He could tell a good story; that's one of the things that attracted me to him. I'd watch him pace himself, embroider the plot, revel in the tale, then deliver the punchline. He'd glow and smile. I was proud of him.

They're still chuckling next door, like their teeth are

scratching the wallpaper, taunting me. They can't leave it alone. I hear the door, he's off to work. There's a snigger through the kitchen window as he walks along the balcony. It must have been a good one.

I take Roy his breakfast. He doesn't say anything, just sits there po-faced as I pull the curtains to let the grey light in. I leave him staring into space. I wash up the breakfast things and water the daffodil bulbs on the windowsill.

I could never tell jokes – too embarrassing. I'd forget the story and start giggling, turn bright red, and look for a hole to crawl into. I like most jokes, but there's a lot I don't understand. It's not that I don't understand the joke but I don't see what's funny. Sometimes they're just hurtful, like racist jokes or nasty ones about sexual perversion. But a good joke's like a piece of timeless magic. I can't remember jokes but I know exactly where it was I heard them, the colour of the wallpaper, a mole on the face of the person who told it, the way someone fell about laughing, gasping for air.

The next night I'm out on the balcony having a cigarette. He won't let me smoke in the flat, not since the doctor made him give up. Three flats along I can hear them laughing, they're in hysterics. It's like a virus is breaking out. They close their window to muffle the laughter. I smile and nearly drop my ciggie down four floors, but I'm curious. What can be so funny?

I go in and sneak into bed beside him, he grunts and rolls over away from me. When we first met, I couldn't wait to sleep with him, to share his bed. I would have given anything, and it was worth it. He was a good lover, passionate and thoughtful. But now it doesn't take much for me to creep out and curl up on the settee with some old film on the telly. He doesn't like me doing it, he likes me there, right next to him breathing the same air.

I've seen this film before, it's a western. When I turn it off I can hear chuckling in the distance, making its way along the corridors and down the stairwells, like bad plumbing. Or am I just imagining it? I can't tell but I fall asleep listening out for more. I'm a child again and Dad is telling me a story, it's sending me to sleep, safe and secure. I sleep for what seems a year, or was it five minutes? Soft laughter from somewhere in the block wakes me.

I get up, dress and go out to fetch his prescription. I bump into the next-door neighbour, Joyce, on the staircase. We exchange greetings, and I pluck up the courage to ask her.

'You were having a good laugh the other night.'

'Don't,' Joyce says slapping my arm, her eyes rolling behind the peroxide fringe. 'Bert came back from work with a cracker, best joke I've heard in years.' I raise my eyebrows in expectation, and she takes a breath. She describes the situation richly, one I can identify with, as most people would. Years fall off her as she acts the part. She looks me in the eye and assures me, describing the scene, building a picture, a place with warm people. I nod in encouragement, fully understanding the character's predicament. She balances carefully on the metal stairs, nail varnish against galvanised steel. I concentrate hard in case I get the wrong end of the stick, listening for anything significant, something that might be twisted, turned round and used in the punchline. She gets closer, her breath is rancid, her eyes wide open. She pauses, then slowly lets the final words leave her yellowing teeth and smudged lipstick. She pushes me away, hard against the handrail laughing at her own joke. I laugh, slowly at first, enjoying the intimacy, our bodies sliding out of control. My stomach muscles complain at this new exercise and tears start to roll down my face. She looks worried, but then she's laughing at my contortions. We are rag dolls hanging on the balcony, falling into each other. Gradually we gain air and inflate, our spines become stiff.

'Mind you, I don't tell it as well as Bert,' she says.

I light a ciggie and offer her one. She lights it off mine, and then asks.

'What about you, have you got one?'

I wipe my eyes and shake my head. She takes a drag of the ciggie then scuttles off like a disappointed dealer. I quickly memorise the joke's form and punchline, thinking about its pace and content.

My father was a travelling salesman and kept a joke book. He said you have to sell yourself and the product follows. If they like you, they'll like the goods, and everyone likes a joke, so that was his way in. His joke book had all his clients entered alphabetically, with their preferences next to their name. Like (sh) for shit jokes more popular up North, (m-i-l) for mother-in-law jokes – widely popular, (sex) jokes – very popular in the Midlands. There was even (ESI) an Englishman, Scotsman and Irishman category, as well as many more. In the different sections the punchline would be written carefully in his tiny handwriting. Before calling on a client he would quickly sift the book and choose a joke to smooth the sale. He carried the book for twenty-two years, and then on his last week of work, he left it in a telephone box in Brighton. Its cracked black leather next to the calling cards of Rita the meter maid and Simone of S&M delights.

That's all I wanted when he died, his joke book, to remember those funny nights by the fire when he would have us in stitches. Roy would copy him and steal some of his jokes. I didn't mind, I thought it was flattery and Roy told them well. But, I never dared tell jokes at home, that was what Dad did, and I wouldn't have dreamt of treading on his toes.

I put Roy's medication in the cupboard and make the tea. I wish he wouldn't watch so much daytime television, especially the news. It just makes him worse. The Middle East and the starving in Africa, what can he possibly do about them?

Again that night I hear laughter rippling though the block. At first it's the mechanical laughter of the TV, alongside hi-fis and barking dogs. But later it's more eccentric, people gasping for air while Roy's fast asleep snoring. I make some hot chocolate then go to the bathroom. I look in the mirror, and I swear if I look hard enough I can still see the girl that wooed Roy, she's still there hiding behind the wrinkles and chins.

I tease her out with some silly facial expressions. She is smiling at me. I remember the first lines of the joke, and say them quietly, keeping a straight face, with just a faint glint in my eye. I recall the gestures, the drama, as the joke unfolds towards the twist, and the pause. She is looking expectantly through the cracked mirror, I take a breath and deliver the punchline with immaculate timing. She laughs with me. I stifle the laughs. I must not wake him. I put on some make-up and lipstick, a dress rehearsal. She looks happy, we are one, confident and charming. I tell the joke again with aplomb, celebrating under the forty-watt bulb and half-tiled wall. Two years I've been decorating the bathroom, but the Tesco job doesn't leave me much time.

After I've made his breakfast I go outside for a ciggie to find courage. I'm on late shift today. Bert from next door rushes by late for work. I wash up first then take him tea by the telly. I tidy the room and disconnect the digital box, but he doesn't notice for a while, then I switch the damn thing off. I place a chair directly in front of him. He looks puzzled. I smooth the folds from my dress and push back my hair.

I just begin, I don't announce it or give a rambling introduction. His face is the colour of pale cardboard but I can see a glint somewhere in those Valium eyes. I'm enjoying it. He is curious, like watching a documentary on the History Channel he can't understand. I'm very slow and deliberate, making sure he follows the important parts that may be destroyed and turned over with the twist. I stand up, more room for gesture and expression. He is impressed but not overcome. I catch a glimpse of Roy at twenty-four, carrying three pints from the bar with a fag in the corner of his mouth. There are tiny red lines in his cardboard face moving blood from that heart I love. I'm gaining, I know what's coming but I mustn't laugh. I pause, then like a full kiss on his dry lips, I deliver the punchline. I chuckle a bit, but not enough to steal the response. I stare into a young Roy's eyes and very slowly they sparkle like a distant shooting star. His face lifts and the corner of his lips turn up. His hands let go of the tarnished armchair and he shakes his head slowly, in disbelief. Then a sound like a depth charge rumbles through his stomach, up his throat and delivers a small but perfect chuckle. He turns to me, with a smile, as his grey face starts to redden.

'You told it well, love. Just like your old man.'

Later that week, as we're walking down the stairs, we pause to let Joyce by. She greets Roy as if she'd seen him yesterday, then winks at me, raising her nail-bitten thumb. She carries on up the stairs, and Roy turns and calls to her, 'We're off to feed the ducks.'

The Autograph Hunter

Keith hitched his football socks up and climbed the stairs two at a time to the top floor of the flats. He wasn't a football fan, but he couldn't be bothered to change after games at school. He clutched the book his mum had just given him after weeks of begging, while she stayed indoors with the man he hadn't seen before.

Breathless when he got to the sixth floor, he stretched to reach the bell and waited patiently. He thought he'd start at the top, flat 28. A silhouette appeared behind the frosted glass panels of the front door.

'Who's there?' it asked.

He cleared his throat, 'Keith, Keith Bolton from flat 10.'

Chains were removed and bolts released. The door opened a few inches and an old woman's face peeped out. Keith didn't want to mess about; he'd got the whole block to do before bedtime if he was going to fill his book and impress the others. At least this gave him a chance to shine; he was hopeless at football. He held the book open towards the woman.

'Can I have your autograph, please?'

A smile spread across her face and the door opened

wider. She started to laugh, one hand across her chest, the other held out theatrically. 'Me? My goodness, you'd better come in.' She had the biggest selection tin of biscuits Keith had ever seen, from thick plain brown ones with little holes in, to ones wrapped in their own gold paper. Autograph hunting was already more fun than Keith expected. Eventually the woman found her glasses, and made space at the table. She took a fountain pen from her handbag and sat upright, Keith watched her staring over her glasses at the ceiling. Maybe she was looking for cracks. Then she smoothed the pages of the book and wrote, 'The world is a wonderful place Keith, enjoy it.' The fountain pen made a scraping sound across the thick paper as she signed it with a bold signature. He looked at the inscription, and wished he could write like that.

She squeezed two golden biscuits into his pocket. 'Come and see me again, Keith.' He knew he'd have to think about that.

At number 27 there was no answer, but Keith worked his way through the block gathering swirly gestures, daubed capitals and spindly insect writing. Everyone would come to their door as if he had done something wrong and they were in the middle of their favourite TV programme. But when he asked them to sign his book, they smiled and seemed to grow an inch or two. They looked at the other pages, curious about their neighbours. His mother's shrill voice echoed through the stairwell, he left an unanswered door and ran down the stairs with his half-filled autograph book.

The front door was ajar, and he crept into the kitchen where the man was cuddling his mother. 'See you babe,' he said, gathering his coat. He rubbed Keith's hair. 'Look after her, Einstein.'

Most of Keith's suppers came out of packets, with pictures of what they should look like on the outside, but they never looked like that on the plate, although they were tasty.

After dinner, his mother sat with him and looked through the autograph book, trying to guess which neighbours were which. She knew them by sight, but not their names. Keith laughed at the ones she got wrong. He knew almost everyone in the flats now and they were all right.

Later that night he took a drawing book from under his bed and turned to the back. There were hundreds of Keith Bolton signatures spread across the sheets, but he couldn't make his mind up which one was really his. He wrote some more with the h of Keith looping round all the other letters. That's what the woman at number 4 did with her name, but his didn't look right. Closing the book he gazed out at the cityscape with flickering colours of TV light filling the windows. He got back into bed and thought of all the people in the houses and flats, and the amazing collection it could provide for an autograph hunter.

The next morning his mother leant down and kissed him, something he didn't like by the school gates. There was a new broach on her cardigan, some kind of insect with a coloured stone in the centre. He wondered if it could bite. In the playground, bags were dropped on the tarmac and small groups huddled around, sharing the latest craze of autograph books. Keith had left his at home; he wanted to fill the book before presenting it triumphantly, and in case the bullies got hold of it.

The crowd was marvelling. 'That's cool,' a tall kid cheered. 'How the hell did you get hers?'

'My sister met her at the TV studios, when they were on a trip,' the boy answered. The others piled in to see it, and Keith got pushed away; he didn't recognise the TV personality's name.

In class his name was read out. 'Keith?'

'Here, Sir.' As other names followed, he wondered about the meaning of fame. Everyone could be famous to him, even the names in that room. It wasn't a proper autograph if you got your sister to get it for you, and besides, that autograph book had hardly any signatures in it.

His mum collected him and drove him home in her old Mini, with its dents and broken wing mirrors.

'We're going out to your favourite, later,' she said.

'But, I've got to finish my autograph book,' Keith protested, 'I've only got six more to get.'

She laughed, 'When you get an idea in your head, there's no shifting it. You'll have to be quick.' They travelled home in silence, Keith dreaming of speechless bullies standing back in amazement, when they saw his collection.

The book was still under his pillow. He grabbed it and rushed to the second floor, ringing bells, disturbing dogs and waking old men. He just managed to get five new autographs by the time his mother called.

'He's meeting us there,' she said. She was wearing bright pink lipstick and started to brush his hair, two more things Keith wasn't fond of. He hung on to his autograph book as they left.

The Wimpy Bar was busy for a Wednesday night, and the man was already sitting at a corner table. He put out his hand to Keith; it was enormous and swallowed his small paw.

'What you having?' the man pointed at the menu.

'He'll have a cheeseburger with chips and a strawberry milkshake,' his mum answered, twisting a finger through a large curl and tilting her head to one side.

Keith felt sure the man would be coming home with them, but at least he'd get to watch the film on TV. The man had a big laugh and Keith's mum seemed impressed, not knowing quite where to look. After they had wiped their hands with napkins and Keith had eaten the last of the chips, they cleared the table, except for the coffees. There was an uneasy silence, as Keith fidgeted with his book.

'What have you got there?' the man asked.

'Show him, Keith. Go on, don't be shy.'

Keith wiped the table carefully with the last napkin,

then placed the book so the man could see it. He read the first autographs with their inscriptions, and flicked through some of the others.

'So, you went round all your neighbours, asking for their signatures?'

Keith blushed and nodded. The man had paused on the last page, but Keith wasn't sure if he wanted his signature. He didn't know if he liked him, but he needed to fill the book. He liked everyone else in it, and could remember the biscuits, drinks and stories that came with their names. But after all, the man had bought him his favourite meal.

'Can I have your signature, please?' he asked.

The man winked at his mum and ruffled Keith's hair. 'Of course you can.'

He took a pen from his pocket and wrote carefully onto the last page, then closed the book and gave it back to Keith. 'Who's for some ice cream?' he asked.

The following morning Keith was up early, and helped himself to corn flakes. He could hear the man whispering in his mother's bedroom. She was surprisingly agreeable when Keith offered to walk to school on his own.

The playground was empty when he arrived, and he sat on a bench kicking his heels while the book waited inside his school bag. After fifteen minutes or so, others started to arrive and the older boys kicked a ball about. Keith turned the pages of his autograph collection, and paused at the man's signature in average handwriting, with no inscription. He closed his bag and tentatively walked towards the larger boys flicking a ball between them and showing off. He knew the Greek boy Panos with glasses, quieter than the others. He approached him slowly, held the book out towards him, and gestured for him to read it. Panos turned the pages and then let out a large laugh.

'Who the hell are these, boy? I never heard of any of them.' One of the lesser bullies joined him and looked, but was equally unimpressed. He threw the book down, and they started pushing Keith around. He tried to pick it up, to run away, but they held on to him. Then the largest bully walked over and grabbed the book. He looked Keith up and down, then opened it at the last page. The snarl suddenly faded from his face, as his eyes got bigger.

'Where d'you get this?'

Keith shrugged his shoulders. The bully was looking intently at the man's signature, 'Jimmy Greaves', written clearly on the cream paper in a blue-black pen.

'He was one of the best, a real Spurs giant, a Tottenham hero.'

'And an England international,' Panos boasted.

'Yeah, and he commentates on TV as well,' the first bully added.

'Where d'you get it man?' He stared down at Keith.

'He goes out with my mum.'

'Wow, cool.' A crowd had gathered around, making sounds of approval and patting Keith on the back. He didn't understand their enthusiasm but was enjoying his new popularity. The bully closed the book.

'You want to look after that, man,' he gave it back to him. 'Want to be in my team?'

Keith nodded, put his bag by the others making goal posts, and ran into the middle of the playground knowing he would never get a touch of the ball.

When he got home the telly was on and he could see his mum had been crying, she didn't want to talk. He never found out if the man was the real Jimmy Greaves, or just another Jimmy Greaves. It didn't matter.

Keith went into the kitchen and took some fish fingers out of the freezer, looked at them, gold and crispy on the packet, then emptied the contents into the frying pan. He would try hard to cook them for her, just like the picture.

Cut Flowers

A copy of *Flower Arranging Monthly* hit the doormat with a sprinkling of junk mail and a letter. Eric picked the magazine up, looked at its cover with a special feature on wreaths, and threw the leaflets away. He took it to the kitchen and put it on the pile of other mail for his wife in case she came back.

There was one letter addressed to him in an official envelope from the MOD. They'd found his son's body. A week later two officers delivered a small bag of possessions. Occasional eye contact was made, the soldiers' hard blue, the father's red but dry.

The tall one spoke first, 'Lovely cup of tea, Mr Jarman. Rare to see tea leaves these days, proper tea.' Eric picked at the sofa arm, exhausted from the months of hoping that they would find his son alive. He had imagined ghastly scenes, and felt the pain of dreamed bayonets passing through the boy's heart, then his own. At night he'd see him blindfolded, humiliated and tortured, then Eric would lay awake helpless staring through the ceiling, the roof and into the stars.

The fat one squeezed a peaked cap between his large

hands and coughed. 'You must be very proud, Mr Jarman. Your son was very brave.' He drained his cup, the best porcelain. 'The regiment will honour him of course, and we will make all the necessary arrangements.' They left some papers with a phone number for a helpline, and vanished just like Terry.

The vicar came to search for Eric's soul and to prepare for a service. Eric had no beliefs but if he did believe in a god it would be an outer-space god or just a cloud. He signed the papers and showed the vicar the way out. Guilt, chronic heartburn gouged his stomach making his days painful, filling his nights with angst.

Eric turned the stereo up and lost himself in a new Ry Cooder album. He'd got it when Amazon told him that customers who bought a Bill Frisell album also bought the Ry Cooder one. It felt safe to be advised. He was imagining a Mexican landscape and dozed off to cicadas and a sea breeze. This was interrupted by a nightmare where Eric was beating his son, trying to knock some sense into him.

Terry, an only son, had joined the army three years ago, preening himself in the hall mirror in full uniform, his peaked cap hiding his face.

'What d'you think?' He stood to attention. Madge and Eric looked at the soldier and wondered where he had come from, as if he had invaded that morning. Madge kissed him and Eric shook his hand; a soldier on parade, a number in a row of thousands. He saluted them, clutched his bag and left for Afghanistan, a place he couldn't even spell.

Eric was partly relieved that he'd gone, unable to show the boy any direction in this foreign world. He didn't know what to do with his own life, relabelled and repackaged too many times to offer advice.

'It'll make a man of him and give him a job in these hard times,' Eric reasoned.

'I'd rather shape him myself than let some sergeant major do it,' Madge replied. But it was Terry's choice to join up, seduced by widescreen adverts in the cinema following bad GCSE results and being jilted by Sharon Gillard after three years. He would come home on leave, each time a fainter copy of the Terry they knew, slowly withdrawing into the uniform, until they hardly recognised him. That's when the big arguments started. Eric wanted him back, but he couldn't say it, could only criticise the boy's immaturity and his naivety in a pointless war. The boy saw it clearly in black and white, not the shaky sordid colour of the television pictures Eric stared at every night. He tried to explain to the boy but his emotions fogged his words.

'You know nothing,' Terry shouted, pointing at his father. Eric lost it, flailing across the room, hitting the boy's face, driving him from the house.

Eric turned the music off. He couldn't understand how he was so alone. He wanted to start again but it was too late. Pacing the house, he searched in drawers, opened boxes, stared at photo albums, losing recognition of the woman and the boy by the beach hut, making sandcastles and running through the waves.

Later that week he ventured out to get some milk and tripped over a separated bouquet. There had been many piled outside the house, with scrawled messages of sympathy. The teenage misfit was now a hero. The flowers looked a mess, pieces of nature, one by one suffocating in their artificial wraps and spoiling the reliable order of Eric's paving. Ever since Princess Diana's death, flowers lived in plastic. He grabbed as many as he could, carried them down to the side door, and stacked them on the kitchen table. He carefully removed the crackling plastic covers and put the wilting flowers in water. Fetching some vases from the dresser he started to make arrangements. He placed them in different rooms where the colours complemented the wallpaper and curtains; Madge would have liked that. He never let her put flowers upstairs, but now the bathroom had a bouquet of miniature roses, and even Terry's room smelt fragrant. At last the table was bare, and Eric hoped that would be the end of it.

He went back to work, in monochrome clothes, and held broken conversations with inquisitive colleagues, turning down their supper invitations. In the evening he became familiar with Indian takeaways, playing with his food, creating patterns on the plate before throwing it in the bin. He tried to rid the rooms of the boy, hiding photos and plastic trophies in drawers, putting his coat, trainers and rucksack into the loft. He was a stubborn ghost.

Slowly petals fell from the arrangements, clashing with the floral carpet. He left them there, grinding them into the pile with his pacing. Brown stalks held firm in cloudy water as their stench filled each room. Sometimes his eyes would moisten, a touch of hayfever, he thought. Their sunken heads took on sepia tones, like old photos of grand bouquets, as Eric lost all sense of time. He played his Ry Cooder, tampering with the graphic equaliser to find the right balance, but it eluded him.

It was a month since Terry's body was buried and more since his wife had disappeared. The vicar had suggested he do something, join a club or get a pet. Eric didn't want any of that, but he wanted to show the vicar he had a soul.

Late that night, unable to sleep, he turned the security lights on and went to the shed. He grabbed all the bamboo poles, accumulated over years, too useful to throw away. Skills he had forgotten controlled his fingers as they lashed the canes with intricate knots, and a giant wheel with spokes started to grow. Eric took the scissors from the drawer and rushed out to Madge's treasured garden. One by one he cut the stalks, hollyhocks tumbled, they would weave well for him. Delphiniums were snipped and carnations picked. Sweat ran down his back as he struggled up the path with his arms full, and colour drained out of the garden. He worked all night, tying flowers into his structure, trying to keep order to the circular spectrum. By sunrise it was a blazing colour wheel outlined in green. He stood back and inspected his creation adding the last touches with wild poppies.

The garden was bare, and Eric stared at the brown earth, shivering. The wheel was as wide as the shed and taller than him. He struggled to manoeuvre it towards the back gate, dragging it across the path to the side entrance where he rested it against the wall. His head was spinning and his arms ached. A sudden gust of wind took the arrangement. It felt much lighter, and sailed through the back gate like a kite. Eric hung on as it turned the corner to the front of the house, falling into place against the fence where the suffocating bouquets had been. It was finished, this was a proper wreath, one to be proud of, a monument.

'What d'you think?' he wanted to ask someone, but there was no one there. He went indoors and collapsed on his bed.

The arrangement drew crowds and the local press, but Eric refused interviews. Neighbours slowed down as they passed and took photographs of his grief, and then they showed their friends. Eric watched through the net curtains as the postman walked up the path and paused before he put a package through the letterbox. It was Eric's birthday, though he'd forgotten. He opened the padded envelope and a CD fell out. John Coltrane, *A Love Supreme*, with a card from Madge. How did she know that he wanted it? He put it in the CD player, turned the volume up high and sat back listening to the beckoning saxophone. He opened the card to read her message, but dropped it to the floor as the first tear ran down his cheek.

The Meaning of Rows

I am fifteen, lying naked on a National Health bed, staring at the hospital ceiling and searching for any defect in its symmetry. On the periphery, I can just make out the floral pattern of the curtains, rose motifs repeated in a grid with bleached petals near the worn edge.

A crowd of white coats watch the consultant closely. It tickles, as his pen moves slowly on the skin above my groin. I want to laugh but grit my teeth as the eyes of the twelve trainee doctors stare attentively at the theatrical line Doctor Guttenberg traces on my body.

'We will make an incision here, access the testicle and pull it down. Then our young man can move to the back of the choir and join the baritones.' They laugh politely and file out in an orderly manner.

It's a conventional NHS ward with a cabinet beside each bed, headphones connect you to the BBC and amateur radio enthusiasts who run the hospital radio station, mainly for themselves it would seem.

It is a tedious routine. Day after day I am surrounded by old men, snoring, farting and talking gibberish through the night, moaning for their loved ones. Nurses wake us early in the morning after they have spent so much time and chemicals making sure we slept. They take pleasure from disturbing our slumber, though soon we reconnect with our dreams. I dream of chocolate and exotic food in place of the anaemic grey trays they wake us with.

It is after such a dream that a short fat balding man appears at the end of my bed, eating a Mars bar. A fine example of someone who has tried to survive on hospital food, and has chosen the vending machines instead. He is a NHS employee, and carries a small box with a handle on the top. Checking the list of names, he stuffs it back into his white coat pocket, then pulls the curtains around the bed and smiles at me.

'Pyjama bottoms down, please.' He breathes these words as if he says them a hundred times a day. Of course I obey, and then lie back worrying. I decide to ask the purpose of his visit, in case he is a hoaxer who has stolen a white coat. He doesn't answer, but produces a cut-throat razor from his box, and pulls his sleeves up. My body flinches, and my legs spring up in protection. He pulls them straight, sniffs, and says it won't take a minute. Applying lotion to my groin, he moves my shrivelling penis with deft skill, first to the left and then to the right, and manoeuvres his blade with the precision of a samurai master. In a moment I am bald. I feel light and airy, and think of school friends mailing me a merkin. A word that made us drunk with laughter after Jones found it in the dictionary: 'Merkin (n): pubic wig'. I imagine a blonde number, and pull up my pyjamas.

'See you mate.' He draws back the curtains. 'It might be a bit prickly after the op, but it won't last long.' He is off to another unsuspecting groin, and he's taken all my pubic hair with him. Perhaps he and his wife knit merkins in front of the telly at night.

I dream some more, before Doctor Guttenburg appears on the edge of my bed. What he is telling me would have anyone on the edge of their seat, but I am in bed and recline awkwardly. I am a haemophiliac, which means I need transfusions of factor eight before and after operations to help my blood clot. The doctor beats about the bush, gesturing impossible signs, but slowly I realise they are a bit short of factor eight. 'Nothing untoward,' he assures me. In fact it provides an excellent opportunity for me to help their research. They are going to give me porcine factor eight – a recent breakthrough and highly successful treatment – though it does have minor side effects. In my adolescent ignorance and missed Latin lessons, I ask where porcine factor eight comes from.

'Pigs, my dear boy,' he says with a curious smile. I swallow hard and imagine the donors laid out on a line of beds, giving blood and waiting for their tea and biscuits. I hadn't missed the bit about side effects, knowing it must be more than snoring and the occasional grunt.

'What does it do to you?'

'Well, that's difficult to answer,' he says, 'but after nine to ten days of treatment you will react, and we will discontinue it.'

'React?'

'Yes,' he says, 'the patients that have had it have reacted in a variety of ways. But, don't worry, we'll keep a close eye on you.'

I look at him but he doesn't really look at me, and starts to smooth the bed cover.

'Any other questions?' he asks as if I've used up my quota.

'What if the testicle operation doesn't work?'

'Of course it'll work,' he says, 'anyway, you can always fire off one cylinder.' He pats my knee, grins and scurries away with his white coat billowing like superman. I exhale and lie back, aware that I am a guinea pig about to receive the blood of a hundred porkers. The treatment would begin the next day, a few hours before the operation. I look at the old man in the next bed, who smiles at me reassuringly. It seems I might have temporarily overtaken him in the patient severity tables, which is reassuring for him. I return his smile and he offers me a chocolate. I take one, thank him and turn over. I think I can smell bacon.

Days drift into each other as my natural clock has been interrupted by the anaesthetic, and most of the hospital becomes a blur with occasional visitors. I am a young man, with a newly descended testicle, desperate to test-masturbate this new equipment and sing at high volume to hear any new cadences. It is several days before I take the opportunity to try it out in the cold, clinical surrounds of the ward toilet, images of the flirtatious nurses float through my mind, and prove adequate stimulus. The test is highly satisfactory, with improved power and excellent performance, so much so that I have to go and lie down afterwards. I don't know if the pigs contributed to the extra projection, but I presume it was the newly descended friend. My chin is no rougher, my chest as smooth and my voice the same, so there are no other immediate benefits. The porcine factor eight treatment continues to help me heal.

That night, out of boredom, I start talking to the old man in the next bed, hoping for some of his chocolate. A man I would have passed a million times in the street, without thinking, but here in hospital with the slow-motion clock, any human contact is reassuring. He is old and frail, but anyone over fifty seems dead to me.

'What do you do?' I ask.

He seems to have forgotten what he does, then he turns to me and says, 'I teach philosophy.'

'How d'you teach philosophy?'

He takes his time to reply, but it is clear he has answered this question many times before, and this has not tired him; on the contrary, he visibly brightens. He explains that he is a Professor of Philosophy at the nearby Oxford University, and has taught the subject for thirty years but of course it is always changing. His brief and eloquent explanation will, after the obligatory long pause, beg another question. I think hard, and look around the ward for some help or confirmation.

Eventually, I ask, 'Would it be philosophy to consider what makes a row of beds? If we turn some of the beds around so they face different directions, will they still be a row, sort of thing?'

'Precisely,' he says smiling, and considers some other aspects of this definition.

'But how do we decide what defines a row?' I ask, annoyed that I have got the gist, but not the complete picture.

'Ah well,' he replies. 'You would have to decide on the meaning of rows.'

On that, he turns over. 'Goodnight,' he says and goes to sleep, leaving me gazing at the ceiling, in a philosophical haze. I ponder the order of rows, the continuous circular row of the sports stadium, where rows could look at themselves. I am doing well, and feel quite pleased until I start to get a headache as if someone has cracked my head open with an axe. This is not caused by my lesson in philosophy, but by my body rejecting a load of pigs. I start to shake and know there will be no more pigs' blood for me. I grip the bars of the bed head tightly as the headache becomes unbearable. I start to yell for relief, and sure enough a drug trolley arrives and I am promised wonderful dreams with the aid of morphine. I don't remember much else, like those parties where everyone gives you knowing smiles for days after, and your antics become folklore. It is heavenly though, with the drug cocktail and my new passport to philosophy I venture into parts of my mind that have been neglected since. It is dark and cavernous with enormous ravines. I am lost but not scared, the man in the next bed is my guide and visionary.

In the morning I come back to earth and have something to eat. I must talk to the professor, to clarify some of my thoughts. They let me sleep, with my curtains drawn, but when the nurses pull them back, his bed has gone. The professor decided he'd had enough of rows. He passed away, while I was high on morphine.

I call for a nurse and have trouble finding my words. Perhaps my voice is breaking. Something amazing has happened to me: I am ready, ready to experiment with shaving, to read existentialist poetry, to drive across Europe on a motorbike, to form my own band and sing in a deep voice. Just then a row of familiar people forms at the end of my bed, my father the tallest, with my mother next to him, and my brother next to her. They look at me sympathetically. 'You can come home now, son,' Dad says.

'Oink, oink,' my brother snorts. My mother slaps him. I pack my bag and follow them out into the wild world.

The Tower

Andor leant against the cold metal of the van and watched his breath form small clouds. Fourteen men huddled together, with twelve languages and little in common except hunger for work and breakfast. He looked at his cracked hands, dry from weeks of working with cement, and rubbed a hole in the condensation to watch his new country. He studied the words on the lorries and the vans, wondering about their meaning. The roundabout had signs on it and the buses were drowned in messages. It was raining words everywhere, even the people's coats were decorated with letters.

The van pulled in to the building site where Andor got out first, then splashed his trousers running towards the café and another glimpse of her. She was slim, a young woman, and as she poured the tea she called him by his name. He smiled at her with a glint of gold tooth, and raised his eyebrows in surprise.

'What is your name?'

'Rose love, call me Rose.'

'Rozzaluv,' he replied.

'No, Rose, just Rose.'

He beamed at her, a name he recognised. 'Rosa,' he repeated, sitting at the front of the café and watching the sun rise. The shadow of the letter E fell on his table, cast by the sign on the window. He traced the letter on the brown Formica with his forefinger.

'Here you are love, that'll put hairs on your chest.' She slid a plate of bacon sandwiches in front of him.

'Heres on your chess.' He smiled at her. 'Thank you Rosa.'

She weaved her body between the tables, dancing for his eyes.

He had been in Britain for six months now. The English people he met were all officials, mostly curt and sometimes bloody-minded.

The motors started turning and hoists moved as the drone of heavy equipment replaced birdsong. He put the safety helmet on, with his tobacco in its inner rim. He had to ration his smokes as the foreman was known to be hard. The site was busy with greedy contractors. It had already been sold several times between property companies, one in Jersey, another in Frankfurt, each taking their profit. The migrant labourers did the unskilled work sweating in the deep foundations, a hole in the earth's surface as if a meteor had hit it. Andor was curious how the English did things, and surprised that they weren't more interested in how other countries did them. Messages were shouted above the noise, clarified by sign language, a universal code with increasing subtleties. Andor knew what to do, but when he didn't, he watched others and copied them. It was rare he made a mistake and the English seemed to like him, often taking him into their confidence, nodding at the surveyors and making masturbation gestures in the air. He laughed and encouraged them. When a difficult task came up he always volunteered quickly as he wanted the work and to do well. He needed money badly for rent and food. He would love to be a surveyor, no matter what gestures he attracted, or even an architect, and then he could send money home. The foreman signed fag-time and Andor climbed out of the ground and back into Rosa's for tea.

He sat in the corner with the others trying to read the headlines in the newspaper. They were bold and filled the page, sometimes bigger than the story, good for Andor to learn. When they had said them out loud a few times they would turn to page three, and look at the plump breasts, dreaming of girls at home. He knew Rosa watched him as he tried to form words, his large hands gesturing to share jokes with the others, to show his ideas. In no time at all cemented boots were dragging back across Rosa's floor, and Andor would catch her eye to say goodbye.

On the site, more instructions would be shouted over the noise of drilling as it echoed off the dock walls. Clueless smiles were shown as a foreman cursed a misunderstanding. It was a big project, head offices for a global communications company, twelve storeys towering on the edge of the waterfront. They were already behind.

Andor was struggling to understand the Geordie foreman, words he thought he knew were foreign from this man's mouth, but his understanding of body language was improving fast.

Day by day, the tower climbed into the sky, an architect's dream of a giant mobile phone, sending messages 24-7, and casting shadows across the old warehouses. Summer brought evening sun, tinting the walls of their hostel orange and tanning their faces. They would sing pop songs from the radio, but Andor would look at books trying to learn new words, and of course think about Rosa. Every night he would go running round the docks, past the tankers and across the park. One night he noticed Rosa standing by the fence. She was wearing a summer dress with a floral cardigan, her hair up with dark glasses, a Hollywood star not a café waitress. Andor was suddenly shy and not sure of himself. He stopped. She smiled and beckoned him. Moving slowly across the gravel he felt dirty, like a schoolboy in his improvised kit, gazing at her through the wire. She gestured towards the end of the fence, and he went out through a gate to join her. Holding up his hands, he apologised for his kit. 'It's not beautiful, I think.'

Rosa laughed, 'I've got something for you.' She took off her glasses, and stroked the hair from her face.

'For me?' he stood back.

'It's nothing really, but I saw you trying to read the paper.'

'The others like pictures, but me, I try to read.' He exhaled heavily. 'Not easy.'

She reached into her bag. 'It's a dictionary, it was my father's.'

Andor took the book from her, holding it delicately. 'You are kind.'

'It's a spare one, it's fine.'

Andor tilted his head.

'You live alone?'

'You could say that.' She looked away.

'I wish I was not with so many. So noisy, all day. You are lucky.'

There was a moment of silence as he studied the cover. 'How many words?'

'I don't know.' She laughed, and watched him scan the pages. 'We don't use them all. You can get by with just a few.'

Andor looked her in the eye and hesitated. 'Would you read to me, please?'

'I'd like that. You can come to my house.' She turned and walked away, towards her car.

Andor ran back along the dock road past the billboards with their huge letters selling cars and beer. He clutched his dictionary and thought of Rosa and her kindness. He was desperate to learn English, to express himself and exchange the time of day. It was hard to meet people without speaking their language. People avoided him, suspicious that he might be a beggar or something worse. With English he could get a better job, a career and financial security. He was tired of being patronised and filling his time with odd jobs.

Sounds of the night filled the bunkhouse, Asian groans and the occasional call for mother in Russian, Farsi or even Yiddish. Andor strained to read the dictionary by the glow from the hall strip light until he fell asleep dreaming of Rosa.

The tower extended its lattice of interlocking blue girders skyward, bound by smoked glass with concrete floor sections and a central labyrinth of cables. Ravenous men rushed to the café at lunch, some taking sandwiches out onto the dock to eat by the boats. But Andor would always eat inside at the table. As he sipped his tea, he noticed a post-it note stuck to the window written in clear handwriting; it said 'window'. Andor repeated 'window'. There were other things in the café with labels on, 'table', 'picture', 'chair', 'menu', 'mirror', 'light', and even the till had a label on it. Rosa had put them there, the same as her parents had done when she was learning. Andor whispered the words to himself, repeating them many times. This was better than the weekly language lessons they were required to go to, where too many played the fool, or showed off until the teacher lost interest. But at least they gave him a notebook. He filled it with words he found in the dictionary, sometimes with small drawings to explain the meanings. He wrote down the words he saw on the billboards, like free, value, more, capital, interest. He looked up their meanings and then looked for other words he wanted to keep for Rosa. Some words seemed to lose their meaning in the adverts, he found them confusing.

Rosa cleared the table and came back with a drink for Andor. The others had gone outside in the sun. She showed him two more labels, one said 'My house', the other 'this Thursday six o'clock'. Andor read them carefully and smiled.

'I'll make you supper,' Rosa said.

'I like that. Thank you.'

Rosa blushed and quickly cleared the rest of the table. Andor made a mental note to bring a change of clothes, he would have to wash in the public toilets on the dock.

Her car smelt of pine, and a small teddy bear hung from the mirror. It was clean and tidy unlike the works van. She drove carefully and Andor watched her eyes flick from the rear-view mirror to the road.

'What age are you Rosa?'

'It's rude to ask a lady's age.'

'Sorry.' He turned away.

'It's all right. I'm thirty-five.' She put a hand to her mouth. 'My god, I'm ancient.' She changed lanes. 'And you?'

'Twenty-six.'

'Gosh, you're a baby.'

Andor smiled and looked out of the window.

He followed her through the gate of the tiny garden to her terraced house. It was loved, unlike the neighbour's piled high with black plastic bags and old carpet. Using her keys in a well-rehearsed sequence, she eventually unlocked the front door.

'Welcome to my home. It's not much but it's mine.' She smiled and he followed her down the hall into the back room, and then the kitchen.

'I'll just check my dad.' Rosa threw her coat down and went back up the hall to the front room. Andor was surprised, but said nothing. He looked at all the books lining the walls. He could tell the type of book by the covers. Romance was everywhere.

'He's asleep.' Rosa put the kettle on. 'Coffee?' She grinned at Andor.

'Your father? He is in the front room?' Andor pointed up the hall.

'He's an invalid, it's no problem.' She grabbed two cups from the shelf. A black cat crept into the room.

'Hello Winston.' She picked him up and stroked him, his purr getting louder.

'You like cats, Andor?' He shrugged his shoulders as she held Winston out to him. Winston struggled out of his arms and slunk away. The kitchen was small with a table for two, squeezed between the units. A noticeboard on the wall had a picture of a young schoolgirl. It was a formal picture, one of hundreds taken that day by a school photographer and sold to proud parents.

'That was me at Foxton Comp, years ago.'

'You're pretty.'

Rosa blushed and got some cake from the fridge.

'That was years ago. God, I can hardly remember.' She got some plates from the cupboard. 'Listen to me going on.'

He moved towards her. It was clumsy but he wanted her. She turned towards him and dropped a tea towel. Her breathing deepened as he edged her towards the wall. Then there was a groaning noise from down the hall. She pushed him away.

'It's Dad, he must have woken up.' She brushed her dress and went to see him.

Andor could hear the groans of an old man, but no words, only Rosa comforting him.

'Don't worry, Dad, I'm here. I've got a friend round.'

Andor crept up the hallway and peeped through the door. The old man was sitting in an armchair, holding her hand.

'You'll be all right, Dad. I'll put the telly on.'

The old man watched her and slurred more words, pointing as she crossed the room. She fetched his paper and rearranged the cushions as music filled the room with the film of an African safari.

Back in the kitchen, Rosa apologised for the interruption and took a tray of coffee into the front room. She sat on the sofa. 'Have you chosen yet?' She watched Andor scanning the shelves taking the odd book down and returning it. Eventually, he chose a large black one, and sat next to her.

'I can't read the dictionary,' she said.

He opened it and pointed to a column. 'I like to hear you speak. Start here.'

She coughed and took a breath then began reading words followed by their meanings. Andor put his hand on her arm, but Rosa moved away. She seemed troubled by the old man mumbling in the next room.

The tower was growing higher with its black reflective windows. Investors demanded more productivity for a quick profit, as shifts stretched and workers toiled. Their English improved as more words and phrases were understood, shouted across the site with a nonchalance that hid their pride. Andor led the team on the roof, taking sections from the crane, directing the driver on the intercom. It was a responsible job, but it gave him some time to take in the redrawn skyline, and to look down on the water's edge. An aeroplane disturbed him, dragging words through the sky on a banner, another advert that he couldn't read. There was a lot he didn't understand, he was becoming impatient, and frustrated by Rosa ignoring him. At night he would think of ways to win her.

The roof took several days to finish. Andor worked in shorts with no shirt securing the final panels, the drips of his sweat left dark spots in the concrete. The project would be finished and some of the men would be moved on to a new project. No one wanted to celebrate the end of the work, but some had bet Andor that he wouldn't see through his plan to impress Rosa.

They led her to the edge of the dock where she could see the tower. The workers cheered as she approached and she began to blush. Andor was poised high on the parapet of the tower. His brown body glistened in the sun, and he looked across the dock and down into the deep water. The men looked tiny with their heads craned back, clutching their safety helmets. Voices shouted encouragement and echoed round the tower. He positioned himself carefully on the edge, remembering what he was taught as a boy learning to dive in Mostar. Elevated onto his toes, perfectly balanced, he stretched out his arms and launched himself into the air. Small as a swallow, falling through the shouts and cries, he cut the water without a splash.

Sentences slipped past, like shoals of fish. Deeper and deeper he dived through words – longer words, words he would never know, words in ancient languages. In the dark depths he saw language that no one could understand anymore. His breath escaped in speechless bubbles, and he pulled himself towards the surface. The underwater silence was broken by cheering workers. He was brimming with new words that he wanted to share, words he kept for Rosa in his notebook.

Cast

Blunt was a boarder and I was a day-boy. Him in the fast lane, me and the others in the slow lane, dreaming at the back of the class and carving our names on the desks. Gorston wasn't a posh school but it was trying hard to impress with a boarding house and gowns. I doubt if Blunt noticed me while he crammed for his exams and got ahead any way he could. Jeffrey was his first name, but Blunt was how he liked to be known, tough and manly. He was more ambitious than me, under pressure with an elder brother in the sixth form. They were close, but very competitive, and Blunt struggled to keep up like an old banger on the motorway. I didn't know much about him, but I saw his dad in Ray-Ban's and a seersucker jacket drop him off once after half term. They didn't hug or anything, his dad just tooted the horn of his silver BMW convertible as he passed through the school gates and gave it some down the street. Blunt went to his mum's for weekends, she lived across town in a big riverside house, and in the holidays him and his brother flew out to the Middle East to stay with their dad.

When I heard that I felt sorry for him. My parents

argued a lot, but at least I saw them regularly, even if I didn't see as much of Dad as I would have liked. He was busy marketing water softeners, driving round the country in a knackered Ford.

'I expect those water softeners are nice. Do they fit them in this area?' Mum used to joke.

'I'm too busy, hun. Anyway our water's not that hard.'

'You ought to hold my hand sometime.'

He'd roll his eyes and go back to paperwork.

I was grateful when they paid for me to go on the school trip to Germany, as they were arguing a lot and I fancied going abroad.

I noticed Blunt was on the list for the trip, and there was an asterisk next to his name, making him an ambassador with extra duties. I was wary of him, flash and physical on the football pitch, confident in a herd of boarders with their codes and customs. They thought they were better, and they were, picking up most of the cups in sports, united in their parentless environment. He ignored me most of the time, especially on the pitch when he rushed past me, six inches taller and built like a tank, but I didn't want it as much as him. When I was drawn to share a room with him I swallowed hard and kept my head down, trying not to catch his eye. But he wasn't looking at me, still hoping he could be drawn with another boarder, or fix a deal with someone better.

'No changes, or deals. That's the draw, boys.' Mr Bateman put his clipboard away and picked up a pile of leaflets.

'Don't forget your information packs, and don't be late for the coach.'

Everyone herded out, excited about the thought of blonde fräuleins waiting for English princes, but I wondered what it would be like sharing with Blunt. My parents were emotional when they dropped me at school, standing by the car, mesmerised, as if they were watching Haley's Comet, not their only son clambering into a school coach. I waved through the dusty window as Mum wiped a tear from her face. Dad offered her his handkerchief, but she rejected it, leaving him to wave the white flag in surrender.

Ten hours later we pulled into the castle grounds just outside Frankfurt, on top of a hill overlooking woodland and the river.

'Lovely tender boys, the Count of Transylvania will be so happy. Let me show you to your rooms.' Bateman took on an amateur dramatic air as the Frankenstein jokes flowed.

I dropped my case on the flecked lino of the small room. He was already lying on the window-side bed.

'All right Pattison? You can put your stuff in the bottom drawers. I'll have the top ones. Okay?'

'Fine.' I started to unpack.

'You don't snore do you?' he asked.

'I've never listened, not while I'm asleep.'

He rolled his eyes. 'You'd get a pillow in the face if you were a boarder and snored. If you do it here I'll set the vampires on you.'

'That's good then.'

I put my clothes away in the drawers and lay down watching him preen himself in the mirror, rubbing his chin.

'Looks like I need another shave. It's never-ending.'

He found his wash bag and looked down, towering over me.

'You don't shave do you?'

I shook my head.

He went into the bathroom and turned to me smiling, 'I've heard they like it rough, these fräuleins.'

I lost myself in a sci-fi book.

Later that night he came into the room carrying a box of beer with a finger to his lips.

'Eight lovely tinnies. Keep schtum Pattison, and I'll let you have one.'

I was jealous that he could pass for seventeen and get booze. The lager cut my throat, and I tried not to cough. He pulled a brand new camera out of his bag.

'Where d'you get that?' I asked.

'My dad. It's a going away present.'

'For you going to Germany?'

'No, for him going to Russia. An apology. We probably won't see him this summer.'

'Sorry.'

'It's not your fault, Pattison. It's my dad's. Anyway he's a cunt.' He reached for another can and threw one at me.

He drank quickly, and talked about long nights in

the boarding house, and his dad. 'It's always the same at Christmas. Turkey, the trimmings, and then it happens. His fucking passport appears on the kitchen table, and we know he's off again.' He crushed a can in one hand. 'That's when Mum gets out the Gordon's, her favourite friend.'

There was a long silence.

'What about your folks?' he asked.

I shrugged my shoulders. 'They're pretty normal I suppose.'

'No such thing Pattison. Nobody's fucking normal. Parents? Pair of runts I say.' He raised his tin and I raised mine. 'Still, we're on holiday aren't we. And here I am getting miserable.'

We swapped some jokes and shared the last can. I washed, got changed for bed and read my sci-fi book. He went to the drawer and pulled out a porn magazine, crashed back on the bed and rustled through the pages till he found his girl. I put my light out, and turned over.

'Night Pattison, sweet dreams.'

'Goodnight, Blunt.'

I heard him get into bed and start masturbating over the picture, fast shallow breaths filled the room, and finally deep gasps as he came. Then his light went out.

I got to know him more over that week, as we investigated the castle and created havoc. We became a bit of a double act. We walked by the river skimming stones. He got one to bounce eight times, but I only ever managed four.

'You're not picking the right stones.' He chose a white

flat stone and passed it to me, but I never threw it. I kept it in my pocket.

That night two German schoolgirls followed us back to our room and Blunt smuggled more beer in, but he turned quiet and shy with the girls. The boarder confidence seemed to drain out of him with every drink, until he was too pissed to do anything. I didn't drink much and got a snog off one of them, and that made him jealous.

When I got home, I gave my mum the ashtray with the painting of the castle on, even though she hardly smoked. She seemed happy with it, and asked if I'd got any photos. I told her I might get some from my room-mate but I doubted if she'd really want to see them.

School started soon enough, and I was looking forward to seeing Blunt again, but when I did he cut me dead. I called after him down the corridor and he raised a hand like he was swatting flies. I couldn't understand it, how you could know someone that well and then just switch it off.

His leg was bouncing like it had an electric fault, just him and me in the classroom after football – I'd tackled him from behind, felled him like a tree and he'd retaliated until there was a brawl. The teacher had left the room and we were supposed to be writing adjectives in alphabetical order. He spat some out, unsuitable ones that we used all the time. I sniggered at them, and watched them leave his mouth in that confident deep voice. We could have been back in Frankfurt. He picked at his nails, whispering. 'Fucking cancer, I hope he gets fucking cancer for keeping us in.' Leaning closer he pointed at my book. 'Go on Pattison, put some adjectives down and I'll copy yours.'

'Why don't you do your own?'

'Can't be bothered.'

My smile widened and I tried to write the list, as a torrent of swear words left his mouth. 'Arsey, fucked, poxy, shitty, spasmo, wanky.'

My pen strayed onto his exercise book cover, where it etched 'Blunt' in small letters.

'What the fuck are you doing?' He grabbed the book and pushed me away. 'You a nonce, or something?'

'I didn't mean to write on your book. I…'

He pushed me onto the ground and pulled my arm up my back, dragging my face across the floor. I pleaded with him not to pull it any further, but he wasn't listening. He wrenched it until I screamed.

The next day I entered the classroom late, with a bright white cast on my broken arm. My mum had said I didn't have to go in, but I wanted to see his face. He was nowhere to be seen. They'd kept him back at the boarding house.

One of the nurses had written 'Best wishes' on the cast, and soon it was covered in signatures, messages and cartoons as everyone left their mark, like I was a celebrity or something. He was away for several days, and there was a whisper about exclusion, but I expected the school needed the fees, so that wouldn't happen.

The cast was removed, and I hung it on my bedroom wall like a big get well card. I was making tea in the kitchen while Dad was reading the local paper.

'Poor woman, threw herself in the river, but left her clothes in a folded pile on the bank.'

I looked over his shoulder at the article and recognised the name. It was Blunt's mum, they had a picture of her, but you couldn't see her face behind the dark glasses.

Dad folded the paper up. 'She probably drowned in the weir.'

I went to say something, but stopped.

'Are you all right, son?'

'Yeah, I'm fine.' I went to my room and passed the bathroom where I could hear Mum sighing and splashing.

I tapped on the door. 'Are you okay, Mum?'

'Yes, love. It's the new water softener. He's fitted it at last.'

I slumped on the bed and stared at astronomy posters on the ceiling, wondering if you could ever get out of a black hole. I turned and flicked open the bedside drawer. It was at the back with some seashells, the flat white stone he gave me in Germany. I clambered through the window, ran across the garden and climbed over the fence. An old man was working his allotment whistling as I ran past him over the rough ground and down the railway bank.

I placed the stone carefully on the line, made sure it was good and sat behind the brambles to watch. The track vibrated, then I heard the train's horn as the huge diesel raced by. The metal wheels of the engine, then the carriages, crushed Blunt's stone, turning it to dust. The passing wind settled and I stood up as the train hurtled west. The powder was ultra fine and I blew what was left of it off the track into the gravel. Kicking the last powder away I followed the line and walked into town. If anyone was around we could spin some stones across the river.

The Archaeologist's Wife

Bill marks out a space in the garden as I watch through the misty kitchen window. I hold my mug, clenching the last warmth, and top it up when he comes in for breakfast.

'Aren't you dressed yet?' he asks.

No good morning, no peck on the cheek, no cuddle. He rushes his breakfast, breaking the shell as he scrapes out the last of the boiled egg with a yoke-stained chin. His feet crash on the stair treads going upstairs, shouting as he goes. 'I suppose you don't have to get dressed, now you've slung in the library job. You'll miss the routine. Still, you know best.' He descends with his new gardening gloves.

'Any chance of more tea?' He tuts on his way out.

It must be serious, if he's using the Alan Titchmarsh gloves, advertised in the *Radio Times*.

We took the Eurostar through the Tunnel for a long weekend last year. It was the counsellor's idea, a final resort. We did the usual things, but he insisted we saw the catacombs, miles of tunnels with skulls and bones. Six million Parisians, stacked in an orderly fashion, like a death supermarket. That's where Bill's mug came from.

New projects start every day, and he's lost interest in the vegetable patch. But he still puts some produce by the road on the little table, for beer money. He wraps them up so carefully in clear plastic bags, all priced in rows by the terracotta jug for the money. It upset him last week. Someone nicked the small change and urinated in the jug, but left the vegetables.

I put the kettle on again, a peppermint tea bag in his mug, and another red label one in the pot for me. I've tried to reach out for him in the night but he turns away, rolling into a ball. It's years now that we've slept in the same bed but dreamt of other people and other places. Our house has become a museum, where exhibits can't be touched and I am on display as a human, next to the carp Bill caught and stuffed when he had his taxidermy phase.

I tap on the window and put his mug outside on the sill. He waves as if he is a tourist in another country. I close the window to stop the draught, and the sound of his whistling.

My mug begins to warm, and I think of Trevor at the library, when he ran his hand up my skirt. We were tidying the storeroom together. The tingle lasted all day. I knew he fancied me, the girls had teased me for months, but I never thought a pass would come, nor what followed.

'Fiction is all very well,' he said, pushing me back across the inter-library loans, 'but I'm a non-fiction man, myself.'

I go back upstairs to dress and open my wardrobe. It still looks like my mother has left her clothes in there, everything old and musty. Even though I went on that shopping spree, choosing colours that I'd never worn before, gaping at the new woman in the changing-room mirrors. The woman who had sex in the library storeroom, interrupted by Madge looking for the kettle.

I remember her trying to smooth things over, with trifle smeared on her fat face, cheeks reddened by bad blood pressure and too much sun. Custard slid down her chin onto her summer dress.

'I didn't say anything to Mrs Pilfrey, honestly Betty.' Her podgy arms lifted some overdue books onto the trolley making more room on the desk for the trifle. She pushed it away, and began to scrape her skirt with an old library card.

'I'm a bit off my food today,' she announced. 'We're still friends, aren't we?'

I nodded, and looked away as she licked the card.

'There's a nice film on at the village hut this Friday, if you fancy it. It's that love story everyone's talking about.'

I wondered if Madge would follow me to the grave, jabbering and grazing. She lost her Ron two years ago, but she still cooks for him in her five-bedroom vicarage, laying the table every night and eating his portion. At least she'll still have her job at the library, something to get up for. Everybody needs to fill a hole.

That Friday, we had tea in her summerhouse with its sofa bed and rattan chairs, hidden by trees at the end of her huge garden. She let me sleep there one night, when I was thinking of leaving Bill, but I didn't tell her that. It was like a treehouse, just me with the owls at night and the flicker of flames from the wood burner throwing yellow across the pine walls. I pulled the quilt around me tight and wished I could have stayed there forever.

We set off for the film early and Madge was excited, handing out large bags of home-made popcorn and telling me all about the film.

'There are two Americans. One's loaded and the other's quite poor. They meet in a hospital tending their sick partners who are dying from cancer. Well, they grieve together and then they re-appraise their lives, and guess what?'

'They have rampant sex in the mall?'

'Not quite. But they do get it together. Touching, isn't it?' Madge put in another load of popcorn, and her eyes dwelt on this story of hope, but only for a moment before the sugar hit.

She grabbed me. 'Come on, I don't want to end up in one of those plastic bucket seats again.'

Leaning across her broken armrest, she whispered, 'I've seen him before, playing a General in Vietnam and she was in *ER* and that sit-com thingy. Are you sure you don't want any popcorn?'

I shook my head. Madge crunched her way through the film, but I couldn't be bothered to follow it. I woke up when the leading lady had to bare all, an advertisement for nip and tuck, and I began to wonder if a bit of Botox might bring Trevor back.

Madge suddenly shrieked and the crowd shushed her. She whispered that the man next to her had tried it on, put his hand on her leg. I looked across to see a seventy-year-old man, struggling to blow his nose. She dragged her chair closer to me. Honey, popcorn and Madge's moisturizer filled the air.

'I wouldn't kick him out of bed,' she nodded at the screen as she regained her confidence. I watched the film star shower and recalled Trevor's arse, fine and pert. But I wasn't going to share that with Madge.

That night I lay in bed, in the coffin position. I don't know if Madge did tell the head librarian, but I had been called into the main office and Mrs Pilfrey closed the door behind me, then proceeded to enforce her power. She made it pretty plain as she peered over her bifocals. 'I think it would be best if you left and used another branch of the library in future, don't you? At least till this blows over.'

Trevor said his wife wasn't very well and made apologies. He was transferred to the mobile library, hard labour in Siberia. Trevor has had me in many places, his car, my car, the library and in a friend's caravan. I wanted to have him here in my own home, in my own bed, or Madge's summerhouse but it won't happen now.

Bill pumps his shovel into the ground. He's been digging for days. The county archaeologists have been excavating just half a mile away.

'Roman ruins or something,' Bill says, 'there could easily be something in our garden.' I can only think of Trevor's body moving back and forth, his coarse stubble against my cheek. I've taken a drug and I want more. I have many years to make up for, and I'm not interested in history.

I notice earth flying up from the hole. I can just see Bill's head rise then fall, like a piston in a steam engine, as clouds of earth puff from its funnel. I put the kettle on, and sense a chill might be coming.

The carriage clock chimes in the front room. A cruel gift to Bill, to help him watch his retirement pass. It'll go the way of most things, lining a shelf in a bric-a-brac shop, next to the old records, love songs that no one has the means to play anymore. I start humming one of those songs, drumming lightly on my mug. But I can't quite remember the tune, and I'm left anxiously tapping.

Through the window, I see more clouds of earth rising intermittently, forming neat mounds around the hole. I don't know what Bill is looking for. Maybe he's tunnelling his way out.

Trevor said we could sneak off, have a weekend away. I told him I'm an all or nothing person. He's not happy in his marriage, and his wife has affairs. He said I should be grateful that Bill isn't like that. But I don't think he loves anybody, not anymore, not even himself. I hold my mug waiting for the warmth. The puffs of earth stop.

The hole is an almost perfect circle with small heaps of

earth surrounding it, hour marks on a timepiece. I stare at Bill spread out at the bottom, face down. He is looking away from me into the ground, one arm raised, waving goodbye. Perhaps his heart has given out, it's been running on empty for too long. I pause, and slowly with my feet push the earth back into its hole, then with my hands. It seems the natural thing to do. The hole is filling, and Bill is almost covered. I push the catacombs mug into the soft soil and start to feel warm again, sweat running down my back, hair sticking to my brow. I stand in the hole and take a deep breath, but find myself pulled down as my ankle is caught by something, clasped in a grip. The earth moves, and Bill's brown face spits out wet soil. He is cursing and I struggle to get up. A shovel hits the side of my face, and a bell rings deeper than Big Ben. I throw myself at him, full length. The gloves are off at last. We roll in the earth, more physical contact in that moment than in the last five years.

A voice calls from the house. 'Betty, are you there dear?'

We freeze and stare out of our hole, as Madge's face peers over the edge. There is a long silence, and finally she coughs and makes her speech into the air.

'I came to say sorry, Betty. I feel awful about what happened. But, it's no good burying these things is it?' She throws something into the hole. I wipe my eyes to see the large brass summerhouse key lying in the fresh earth.

Spectacles

I drove through the night, propelling myself towards the coast, in a repetitive ritual rewarded with a full breakfast and a sea view. Here I struggle to read an old newspaper with my broken glasses and give up to walk the front. Some of the shops have survived, even the old opticians beside the chapel. I struggle with the stiff door and push my way in. He sits me in the chair, pulls down the blind and switches on an illuminated test card.

'Make yourself comfortable. I won't be a minute.' He arranges some lenses in a small box and hums a tune. 'On holiday?' he enquires. I nod, and try to adjust to the darkness. Staring through the receding letters into my past, I remember how difficult holidays and journeys were for my family.

Squashed in the back of the car by excess baggage, I gripped the vinyl seating of the Ford Anglia. My mother was driving faster than normal, red slipper pressing on black accelerator. A small squeal of tyre protested on the corner of worn tarmac. My father was crouched in the passenger seat, willing the car to the railway station to connect with

London, then Southampton and the ship that would take him cruising on the Mediterranean. One slip in this chain of travel and there would be no photos of quoits and deck lounging to show when he returned tanned and cocky. Gravel slid as my mother swerved into the station drive, where a youth in a yellow Mini was speeding around the empty car park like an angry wasp. Pressure built as my father simmered and my mother idled. The youth revved his engine and Dad rolled down his window.

'Can't you get out of the way? Some people are trying to catch a train.' Dad's finger tapped his head repeatedly with a gormless expression before he finally bawled at the youth. 'This is a public highway.'

Wired and ready, the youth threw open his door and jumped out of the car. He headed towards us as I made myself very small. He stood tall by the car door, but Dad sat tight and spat words out of the window.

'You're blocking our path, I'm in a hurry.'

The fist moved quickly, one flash of muscle twitch and it passed through the open window smashing my father's spectacles, crashing his face against the headrest.

The wasp sped away burning rubber. My mother tried to comfort Dad but her heart wasn't in it. We watched him struggle across the gravel bound for Cannes, dragging bags and trying to nurse his blackened eye. The train pulled away, Mum put the radio on and we ambled home.

Two weeks later, he returned with glossy photos of himself reclining on deck in Bermuda shorts, matching shirt and huge dark glasses. Incognito, wasp-stung Casanova licking his wounds.

A different lens passes in front of my right eye. 'Can you see that?' he asks. I can smell the optician's bad breath as he moves his large mass around me; there is some clarity to the picture.

'You brought good weather with you, for out of season.'

I watch the letters start to make more sense and read them out as he swaps lenses, and throws me back into a blur.

My mother retaliated by visiting a friend in Majorca for three weeks. She used to dance with Michelle on the stage before they found husbands. Weeks of packing rehearsals and learning 'please' and 'thank you' in Spanish before we drove to Heathrow and put her on a flight into nostalgia that would be too hot and sticky, with a newly teetotal Michelle and no old dance routines.

At home Dad and I struggled with scrambled egg and surrendered to the wonders of takeaway. On the third day, I was at school and Dad was at home servicing his car. Leaning across the engine, he caught the battery wires causing a minor explosion. Luckily his good looks weren't harmed, but his eyes were coated in battery acid. He drove my mother's car through blurring eyes to the local hospital and was whisked by ambulance to the Wycombe General, then to Stoke Mandeville where specialists saved his sight.

The following week he was home wearing large box

type glasses, solid black like celebrity car windows. I had no idea what was going on inside his head.

We arrived to meet my mother at the station, Dad arranged his bow tie and brushed his jacket. I collected the luggage and watched her sunburnt legs skip to the car and Dad.

'What the hell have you got those silly glasses on for?' She peered into the black glass, he grinned back at her conjuring the story he would tell over supper.

The optician holds a light to my eye.

'It's always good to carry a spare pair. We do a deal, second pair half price.'

I keep quiet and stare into the light. He goes to another drawer and puts more lenses in front of my left eye. I can see nothing.

'One pair will be enough, I think.'

Dad lay on the beach, a significant distance from us, huddled round the picnic box on the blanket. Mum knitted a roll-neck pullover for me in maroon. He stretched out, burning under the Cornish sky with his gold-framed glasses resting by his unfinished thriller. Trotting down the promenade, I escaped to the gift shop, with the cut-out models in swimming costumes wearing pasted smiles. I was bored, clutching the ten-pound note that represented months of saving. It was burning a hole in my pocket and propelled me towards the ice cream kiosk.

I swaggered back holding a triple cornet of chocolate, vanilla and strawberry.

I noticed my dad running like a madman through the sunbathers, pointing and shouting at a large gull. Hands shaded bathers' eyes as they watched the bird head for the cliffs with my father's gold spectacles sparkling in its beak. The higher it flew, the louder he shouted and the more people were disrupted. I hid behind the beach huts and licked my way to heaven.

'These should tide you over till the end of the week.' He hands me a temporary pair of black-framed glasses. He mops his brow and battles to tuck his shirt into his trousers.

I make my way to the sea in my new spectacles and walk the same beach where my father left those frantic footprints. Could that passing gull be related to the thief that snatched his gold frames?

It doesn't take many paces before my mind turns to thoughts of my own children and I tighten my coat against the prevailing wind. I realise I never worried about my parents who loved me in their own way. Have I done any better? God knows. The wind blows harder and the sea crashes throwing spray onto my lenses. I walk on and a mist clouds my vision, but I don't bother to wipe the glasses.

Shared Drive

I watched through the window as Mrs B pulled weeds like bad grammar from her convent girls' essays. She was tidying the six-inch gutter of gravel that ran between our concrete drives towards the garages with roll-over doors. I was in the middle of Middle England, standing next to my father's desk needing a cheque for college.

'I hope you're going to make something of this.' He surveyed the invoice.

I rubbed my shoe awkwardly up the back of my leg.

'Concentrate, when I'm talking to you.'

I shrugged my shoulders.

'Well, are you going to make something of it?' He turned and peered into my face. My eyes screwed up under the bright beam of his stare.

'Well?'

I nodded.

He turned his chair round to get comfortable. 'When I was your age, I wanted to do something, be somebody.'

'So what happened?' I interrupted the monologue. The words had only just hit his soft spot when his hand hit my face. In the same way those words had left my mouth, so my body threw itself at him. I held him tightly, to stop any more blows. This had never happened before. I was tired of reprimand, tired of being called a failure. I could hear his heart beating as we struggled on the floor and he tried to wrestle free. I stared at the photograph of Mum in Cornwall, dusty on the mantelpiece. She was as much use there as she was now, dead. I loosened my grip slowly, and through the sobs I shouted, 'Never, ever, hit me again.'

He was shaking and pushed me away as the phone rang. He let it ring for a while, then coughed and answered it. 'Missenden 4532, Vic Widdas speaking.' A perfect BBC weather forecaster's voice, with only a slight tremor of fear. It was an amazing trick, a complete change of person. He was a chameleon, a salesman who had traded his identity.

I went to my room and put some Bob Dylan on, loud. He didn't understand what art college was or why I was doing it. But he showed the occasional visitor to my room, standing proudly next to my latest creation, trying to warm himself in reflective glow. I liked that, but sometimes it got too much for him and me. He couldn't let me dream, or have time doing nothing as he called it. But he had dreams, restoring an old Jag in the garage, listening to his Hammond organ music.

The next day I got a lift back from college with Sam in his old jeep. Mrs B was weeding the front garden, her day off from teaching English at the girls' private school. She was a spinster and lived alone, a Catholic, the object of a lot of Dad's jokes I chose to ignore, mostly double entendre and blatantly sexist.

She watched me as I got out of the jeep. 'Home early, James?'

'Yes, Mrs B. Loads of homework, though.'

'That's a shame, on a lovely day like today.'

Sam stood by the jeep, lank hair hiding his face. There was a smell of petrol.

She looked disapprovingly at the vehicle, then smiled at me.

'The back lawn could do with a mow, James, when you've got some time.'

'Sure Mrs B.' She kept her back lawn immaculate, a green carpet without a weed, hidden by a high security fence and gate. She paid me well to run a mower over it now and again, and it helped towards my driving lessons.

After we'd had a smoke in my room, Sam said he had to get home, to go to a private view in London. His dad was John Piper, a famous artist, and he was having an exhibition in Piccadilly. Out on the drive, the jeep wouldn't start, it just gave a nasty grating cough, until it didn't make any sound at all. He left it there and got the bus. As I watched him rush down the street, I saw Primrose strolling home. I'd been at school with her and we'd both ended up going to art college. She had a boyfriend. He was the son of her dad's boss and wore a brown suit, but I never thought Primrose was sure about him. We'd kissed the week before, and I could still taste her lipstick, a sweet mint flavour. She kissed lots of blokes, when her boyfriend wasn't around. She stopped and gave me a big grin, 'I'm bored James, art history sends me to sleep.'

I stared at her lips. 'I know what you mean.'

'What you doing now?' She was chewing something.

'Photography, for my project.'

She stopped smiling. 'See you later, dreamy boy.' She walked on by, swinging her bag, down to the corner.

I mowed Mrs B's lawn, and sprayed some pesticide where she told me to. She made me a mug of tea, a picture of Windsor Castle printed on it, with a doughnut on a matching plate. Her hand was shaking, her health was worsening.

She slumped in a wicker chair. 'I hear there's been some trouble with drugs at the college.'

I shrugged my shoulders and bit into the jam of the doughnut.

'There's some rough types there. I hope you're keeping well away from them.'

'Try to, Mrs B.' I put the pesticide back in her garage, and washed my hands before the driving lesson.

'Is that jeep going to be on the drive for long, James?'

'I think Sam'll get someone to pick it up soon.'

But he didn't. One garage man came and laughed, offering him scrap value, and it stayed on the drive for weeks after that.

Dad was ignoring me, and was out a lot, but at least I could play my music loud. One night after college, I had a drink with Primrose. We walked home together, it was a hot summer's night and she was wearing strawberry lipstick.

'Take me somewhere nice, James. Somewhere special.'

There was only one place I could think of. She had one of those wrap-around dresses, fashionable at the time. It opened out perfectly on Mrs B's lawn, a blanket of purple against deep green. I knew we wouldn't get disturbed as Mrs B went to bed early and slept like a log with her medication. Primrose wasn't wearing any underwear; white flesh called me. I was helpless. She knew she could do anything with me, even if I thought it wasn't right. It happened very fast.

'Easy tiger,' she whispered. I couldn't get enough strawberry lipstick or Primrose.

I didn't see much of her after that, I tried to phone her but she never answered. I always mowed slowly over that piece of grass. I did more gardening for Mrs B as her condition got worse. Eventually the convent told her they didn't need her anymore.

I got back from college that afternoon and I noticed Dad's old boots sticking out from underneath the jeep, accompanied by groaning noises. There were old parts scattered across the drive. We hadn't been talking for what seemed ages.

I peered under the chassis, to see an oil-stained face.

'What are you doing, Dad?'

'Sam asked if I could do anything with it. I said I'd have a look.'

I watched as he tightened bolts, his face straining.

'He'll be well pleased if you can mend it.'

'I mended hundreds of these in the desert. I think I can fix it, now I've got the parts.'

'Tea?' I asked. He nodded and gave me a smile.

I got up to see Mrs B coming out of her house. She was wearing a headscarf and looked pale as she doddled across the drive with her stick. 'Where's your father?'

'He's under the jeep.'

I went in, knowing she'd come out to complain about it again, and suspected Dad wouldn't be too charming. I watched her through the window pointing at the wreck. Dad cursed as he knocked his head sliding out from under the engine. Mrs B waved her stick, pointing at the spare parts. He didn't like people interfering in his life. I took my time over making tea, and when I went out again, Dad was looking sad as she lectured him.

'It's unsightly, and it's been weeks now. Things like this affect the tone of the neighbourhood.' Mrs B was red-faced as she leant on the jeep door. When she had finished, my father rubbed his chin, and then ran his rag across the wheel arch. He moved slowly in front of the jeep, and smiled at her.

'Would you know of an artist called John Piper, Mrs B?'

She looked at him as if he had insulted her family.

'Of course I do, he did the stained glass windows at Liverpool Cathedral, my home town.'

'Well, this old Willis jeep,' he patted the bonnet. 'It belongs to John Piper.'

Mrs B took a step back.

'In fact, between you and me, some of those stained glass windows were carried in this jeep; the early test ones, that is.'

Her jaw dropped and she tottered slowly round the vehicle.

'Him being a Catholic as well, I thought you might be interested.'

She wasn't listening anymore, but made her way around the camouflaged jeep and came to a pause by the passenger seat.

'May I?' She steadied herself. 'I feel a little faint.'

'Be my guest,' Dad replied, putting his mug down. 'Get in the driver's seat, son, and push that pedal when I tell you.' I leapt in. He pulled hard on the starting handle, and the jeep kicked into life as I pressed on the accelerator.

'Not too much,' he shouted, 'but keep the revs up.' He went into the garage, came out with some L-plates, and tied them on the bumpers. I wasn't insured, but I wasn't going to miss out on driving the jeep.

'Would you like a ride in John Piper's jeep, Mrs B?'

She nodded at my dad. 'Does James know how to drive this?'

'Of course he does,' Dad answered, leaping into the back.

We roared up the drive. I heard her laugh as I pulled out onto the road, and wind blew summer through her thinning hair. I took it steady through the estate, down past the bigger houses with their own drives where Primrose lived. As we neared her house I noticed her outside with a student from college, they were holding hands like it meant something. I slowed down to wave but she ignored me. I rammed the accelerator to the floor and we shot forward. Mrs B's head was thrown back as the wind took her scarf up into the sky. It hovered over us like a new flag for an undiscovered country.

Petrol

James strained to undo the cap, a rusted thread that eventually eased, letting one of his favourite smells out of the can and into the air. He breathed it in, looked at his dream city with the tower still glowing from his earlier attempts with his mother's matches. Slowly he tilted the can over the egg-box buildings. Truthfully, he wouldn't remember much more. Except the explosion that made his city seem pathetic, with fire that came from a different world. The can shot across the garage, and James noticed his new trousers were on fire. He ran into the bungalow, knocking on his father's door where he was on the phone flattering a customer, and James waited outside on fire.

'You must excuse me, Mr Howard, but something's cropped up. I'll ring you tomorrow.'

His father poured water over his trousers and they ran to the garage to extinguish the last bits of the corn flake box houses. James felt the crisp, burnt man-made fabric against his leg as his father held him close, stroking his head. It was strange that when James thought his father would go ballistic about something, he would be kind and loving.

They lived in a bungalow. 'Easier to clean,' Susie, his

mother, said, making simple hoover trips around the ground floor. But James envied friends with banisters to slide down, and stairs to count on the way to bed. Bungalows were large coffins to him, a place to live before you die, full of sleeping parents. He wanted more adventure as an only child, but he owed his father from his brush with arson.

James sat at his father's old bureau holding on to the pen, gripping his hand tightly.

'Four gallons, that's g-a-l-l-o-n-s,' his father said standing over him, Sunday pipe in hand. 'Not too neatly. Be a bit quicker.'

The pen moved with a flourish as James started to enjoy this act, unaware of its fraudulence. This happened once a month, when his father claimed expenses from the insurance company that employed him as a commercial traveller.

'That's fine, just add petrol, p-e-t-r-o-l, nice and small underneath, and put a five in the pounds column on the right.' James stuck his tongue out of the side of his mouth, concentrating hard, hoping to impress him. He could just read the garage name, P–E–G–A–S–U–S; it wasn't a word they had shown him at school, but he liked the picture of the horse with wings. It was a nice little pad, handy for drawing on.

'That's enough now Jim. Well done.' He turned to James's mother. 'Look at that Susie, he's a natural forger.'

'Yes, and who made him one?' she asked.

He changed the subject. 'I've driven five hundred miles this week, up and down that new motorway.'

'Surprised you don't go and live there,' she said, preoccupied with her knitting, not looking at James's father or him, though he pushed his chest out to seek approval. A cigarette hung from her mouth, the ash longer than the cigarette, a trick that always impressed James. She turned to him as if something wasn't quite right, the way she did when he told a fib. Maybe she felt left out, but he didn't worry. She smiled, and tidied his hair. His father eased himself into the armchair, lit his pipe, and vanished behind a small cloud of smoke, leaving the aroma of tobacco to fill the room.

James eventually left home to study geography in a northern town, where they said things in odd dialect, more frankly than he was used to. He would hitch-hike from a service station on the motorway and revel in the adventure of travelling companions as they sped up north away from the bungalow to new horizons. The motorway was a meeting place for him. Lorry drivers, doctors, musicians and writers told their tales with theories about life, offering him pearls of wisdom as they broke the speed limit. He watched their dashboards glow in the night, as he listened to a potpourri of music tapes and confessions. He got a 2.1 and a job in a comprehensive in Norwich trying to locate boys in the geography curriculum while they dreamt of girls in distant places.

Eventually his father retired from the insurance company, and hid his driving gloves away in a cupboard. He seemed lost, taking casual jobs to pass the time. One job involved driving handicapped children to school in a local town, and many of the children were Asian. His father had always been suspicious of foreigners, fearful of their culture and what he did not know. But these children warmed to him like the grandchildren he never had, cuddling him and laughing in the back of his car. He kept a supply of sweets in his glove compartment, and wished he could do more for them, but eventually he got a job in a local garage.

James looked down from the top deck of the bus as it pulled into the market square, and saw his father serving petrol. It was one of the rare weekend visits and he took his time watching his father wipe the windscreen of a young woman's BMW, then pat her young son's head. He seemed proud, happy in the job, guiding the woman from the forecourt as if he had sold her the car. James got off the bus and approached him; they shook hands and wandered into the small kiosk. His father started out on a recollection, paused halfway, to look James in the eye. He shook his head as he realised he was repeating himself, like a music-hall artist, low on material. James wanted to hold him, reassure him, but they turned off the illuminated signs, locked up the kiosk and headed for a drink. They always went to the same pub, where his father had many acquaintances, to share jokes and break the solitude. The Ship was a small pub with low ceilings, beams and well-spoken Middle England voices. James bought the drinks and they sat in the corner, unusual for his father who liked to prop up the bar. They stared into their drinks seeking something. James watched him fidget with a beer mat, his damaged left forefinger a short stub, the tip lost loading a lorry in his twenties. Not thinking fast enough, he had let the lorry leave taking his fingertip to Paris. He put the beer mat down, steadied himself and said he might be going on a cruise, which was not unusual as he did this occasionally. But this time, he said, he would not be coming back. James sipped his beer, wiped the froth from his mouth, then spoke with youthful clarity. 'You only get one father, and I wouldn't want to disown him.' He would miss him, and he was worried about his mother already fading with dementia. His father didn't go on that cruise, but watched Susie leave him slowly, waving forever on an endless railway platform.

James had been to a conference in Milton Keynes, 'Exploring the new frontiers of secondary education', but he'd got lost on the ring roads trying to locate MK7. He'd felt unwell and made apologies before leaving early. There was no rush to get back to Norwich and his wife, he should take it step by step. The hard shoulder was an unfriendly place. He kept calm watching vehicles scream by, eager for destinations, but cursed himself for not reading the petrol gauge and daydreaming.

The six-lane road lay out in front of him, neat and

orderly as far as the horizon. He was buffeted by the draught of large vehicles and deafened by the drone of engines and rubber against tarmac. The motorway slowed, like an air block in a pipe. Two lorries, close together, nearly blew him off course. He paused and watched the huge letters E–U–R–O–P–A–X billowing above the foreign plates. This road led to so many countries, blurred into one. National anthems had lost their resonance, and flags looked more like bunting. It was illegal to stop on the motorway, in this non-stop world with no time to dream. James paused by a pile of fag ends and cans dumped into the giant gutter. He watched the plastic sheeting wrapped around a sorry tree, flapping like a blank flag, trapped in the verge. He spat, cleared his throat, and tried singing to raise his spirits, a tuneless anthem that was drowned out by the noise.

The motorway had recently been widened, but cars and lorries had spread across it, filling every lane like an endless supply of traffic. A bright sign shone in the east, a star above a garage beckoning him. He was glad to leave the noise and started whistling. In the station he chose a red petrol can and asked if it was okay to fill it, then pay. The till worker looked curious, but kept chewing, and nodded. James got the fuel and came back in to warm a meat pasty in the microwave oven, while he flicked through the pages of a road atlas left on a table. The blue and white motorway lines were netting the country, so many more than that first motorway his father drove down. James grabbed a chocolate bar and paid, then turned round to face the traffic. The walk back would be easier, but more frightening as beaming vehicles hurtled towards him.

Dusk was falling on the motorway as headlights dazzled him. A juggernaut pulled over, a quarter of a mile ahead. The driver leapt out, scaled the verge and relieved himself over the hill before scurrying back to his cab. Now he was driving towards James and gaining speed. He threw himself onto the verge and scrambled to the top to catch his breath. The motorway was like a metal river with an ebb tide speeding home. Fairy lights flickered as far as he could see. He thought of his father, old, grey, somehow transparent, and then the funeral. The oldest ritual that was foreign to James. He had never had pets, no rehearsal burying the rabbit, dog or cat. It was a soulless crematorium with a list of the dead, like a Berni Inn menu. Unrehearsed and unresolved he had kept his father's ashes in the glove compartment. The house had gone, his mother in a home. He didn't know where his father belonged, except everywhere, a commercial traveller pushing insurance.

He reached the car, emptied the can into the tank, and put it in the boot. The traffic got heavier and he breathed the air of spent fuel. Then, without thought, he got the urn from the glove compartment. He kissed its cold metal surface, carefully removed the lid, and threw the ashes up into the sky. The wind took them in all directions. They found homes on holidaymakers' roof racks, open wagons, and lorries bound for faraway places. James smiled, eased himself into the car and put some music on, Tamla Motown.

As he pulled into the slow lane, a small cloud of ash rose from the windscreen, hovered above him, and dropped away.

To Catch a Marlin

'What's got your goat?' asked Rosemary, edging closer. Jill kept her distance. The dirge of organ chords muffled the coughs of elderly relatives. They sat patiently through the service, kept their heads down and made mental notes for their final scores. Jill knew this would be the last funeral she came to. She had recognised the photograph of her old lover on the service programme, and felt a flush of guilt as she remembered their illicit meetings. Her mind drifted to her husband Desmond and his headstone casting a sharp shadow in the Caribbean sun. He left her years ago; he had his reasons. At first it was the pressure of work, his shifts on the boats, but Jill got used to that and filled her time with motherhood. Then the trips got longer until she rarely saw his checked coat hanging on the kitchen door, and she had time to fill. They never said goodbye.

'Out of ten?' Rosemary asked as she squeezed herself into the Nissan Micra. Jill turned the ignition key. Her fine eyebrows furrowed as she pondered. 'Six and a half,' she said, 'seven without the condescending tribute.'

Rosemary put her finger to her throat pretending to choke. 'He was a rock we leant on, a pillar of our community, the cornerstone of Geraldine and the family's life.' She took her scarf off. 'They must have got that out of a Christmas cracker.'

'And a cheap one at that.' Jill revved the engine and crashed it into first gear. Rosemary bit into the remains of an egg sandwich. She struggled with her weight – mainly carrying it around. Hypochondria had replaced any chance of weight loss and the condition of her knees was more likely to be affected by astrological prediction than any sensible diet. Jill was the opposite, thin as a rake after years of living on her nerves, a single mum and manageress of the haberdashery department in the local co-op store.

'Well, I hope they pick a better one of me,' Rosemary tutted, as she looked at the photo of the deceased staring out from the service programme. She threw it onto the back seat. They had often discussed the ethics of the funeral photograph, Rosemary preferring to see the deceased in their best light at any age while Jill didn't mind a recent photo, as long as they weren't actually dead. But she knew that when she looked in the mirror she saw anything but her real age.

'Scotch egg?' Rosemary held half in Jill's direction who shook her head violently, trying to negotiate the town's new one-way system.

'You'll bloody disappear if you don't eat,' Rosemary blurted with her mouth full.

They climbed the hill out of town and left the boarded amusement arcades behind them, passing the last fish and chip shop as they looked down on the derelict pier. This was where Jill had spent afternoons with the deceased under the boardwalk, on the old tartan blanket, until someone told Desmond.

'Coast road or bypass?' she asked, clasping the velvet steering wheel cover like a schoolgirl on the dodgems.

'Coast road,' Rosemary shouted and saw the panorama change from hypermarkets and exhaust centres to woodland and the hill climb that would eventually lead to a sea view. Jill's car, better known as Victor — after her late dad — strained to make the final ascent.

'I miss my old Mini,' Rosemary said between mouthfuls. 'You're lucky to have Victor.'

'You could easily get an old banger.' Jill said no more. Rosemary was tight with her money, though well off. She missed many things, children, family, her past. They immersed themselves in a safe silence, aware of their childhood footprints all around them. Blackberry picking from their bicycles, kite flying from the cliff top and their first kisses and gropes in the dunes. They pulled into the lay-by at the summit and both exhaled as if they had conquered each peak on foot. Rosemary slackened her seatbelt, undid her grey duffle coat and spread herself across the reclining seat. It was a fresh October day with clear light around the row of coastguard cottages further along the cliff. The wind clattered the car and Jill delved in the back for her thermos. She poured two cups and peered through the dirty windscreen out to the rough sea. Jill had books with pictures of men braving the wild seas to save ships in trouble. She wished one of those men would come and rescue her now.

'It never fails to get you.' Rosemary looked out across the coruscating waves, billions of gallons of water swirling and crashing beneath their feet. She rolled her window down an inch and watched Jill craft a joint in her baccy tin, adding a medicinal measure of cannabis. She took a deep drag and offered it to Rosemary.

'It's not a strong one is it?'

Jill shook her head and blew smoke out. Rosemary took a tentative drag, and passed it back. 'Quite nice. Different to last time.'

'Home-grown, Sonya's first crop.' Jill took another drag. 'Good for the arthritis.'

Rosemary half closed her eyes and continued sharing the joint.

Before them lay their jumbled town locked in a time warp of all-day breakfasts and boarded-up amusement arcades. Their Victorian school stared out to sea with its arched windows, where they'd learnt their alphabet and how to avoid bullies.

'I wonder what happened to Charlie Stretton?' Rosemary stifled a cough. 'With his groping hands.'

'And the breath of a donkey.' Jill took a deep drag.

'Rumour had it, he was hung like a donkey.'

'With the brains of an ass.' They both giggled.

Jill leant on her steering wheel, staring out at a container ship cutting a line across the horizon. The same type of ship that bought Desmond to her with his bright eyes, disarming smile and curly hair. All she had now was the house, his old fishing tackle and too much time to think. She popped a cassette on and Jimmy Cliff announced he could see clearly now.

'Well.' Rosemary stared out to sea. 'We can't complain, can we?'

Jill didn't answer and kept her eye on another cargo ship, wondering where it was going, and if she would ever travel again. She relit the joint, inhaled, and noticed a small fishing boat near the groynes with a lone fisherman. Desmond was always fishing, forever going on about the marlin in Montego Bay. And the big one that got away. She used to go fishing with him, mainly off the pier. She offered the joint to Rosemary who declined politely and watched Jill drift off.

'Dreamer, where've you gone?'

'Nowhere, that's the trouble.'

Rosemary opened her window and watched gulls circle and pick up the crusts of her sandwiches. Her mind dwelt on all her past desertions, and the minor benefits of dancing alone as she remembered the discos with Tamla songs and sweaty hair.

'You were lucky, Jill. Men wanted you.'

Jill laughed. 'You didn't miss much.' She recovered the funeral programme from the back seat and looked at the lost lover. She screwed it up into a ball and threw it out of the window, where the wind took it high over the beach huts and out to sea.

'I should have done that years ago.' She closed the window.

'What are you on about?' Rosemary delved through her handbag looking for sweets.

Jill adjusted the heater to max and Rosemary popped a boiled sweet into her mouth and bit into it, feeling the sherbert rush. The October light was fading and slowly the ships changed from grey silhouettes to Christmas decorations twinkling out of view.

The following week Jill went round to Rosemary's where she was watching an old *Top of the Pops* on the telly, slumped on the sofa like a marooned whale. She'd ballooned in the last few years, from comfort eating, worsened by her loss of faith when they appointed a gay vicar. She'd never had kids, though she'd brought enough up as a primary school teacher. It was more confirmation for Jill that there was no god if he could be so cruel. Jill perched on the sofa arm and watched a nodding Gerry Rafferty waiting for the saxophone intro to finish so he could start singing 'Baker Street'. She felt the hairs on her spine rise.

'This was one of Desmond's favourites, wasn't it?' Rosemary pointed with salsa dip finger.

Jill nodded, and found the old mother of pearl lure, in her handbag. She thought of his old fishing rods and the bivouac they shared. It was buried under furniture now in her loft, gathering dust. Rosemary switched the television off and poured herself a glass of coke.

'I found a photo of the three of us, having a picnic. But I thought it might upset you.' She put her glass on the rubbish-strewn table.

'Did he ever take you to Jamaica?' Rosemary asked.

Jill shook her head.

'Too hot for me, over there. I got heatstroke in Felixstowe, last year.'

Jill carried some plates out and looked at the piles of dirty crockery in the sink.

'I'll just wash these up,' she shouted.

'Leave it Jill, I'll do it later.'

By the time she had finished Rosemary was fast asleep and early November fireworks lit the night sky.

Back at her house, Jill leant the stepladder against the hall wall and clambered into the dark loft with a torch. Its beam found the old fishing rods and reels in their cases, coated in a fine layer of dust. She took the box of tackle and opened it in the hall. It was his old collection of lures, flickering in the light with rainbow stripes and unforgiving hooks. She closed the box and fetched all his rods from the loft. Over the next few days she used eBay to sell everything for good money, but she kept her favourite lure with its iridescent shine.

They didn't attend any more funerals; Jill's heart wasn't in it. She had apologised to Rosemary, and felt slight guilt as she stood outside the travel agent clasping the wad of notes.

He was the only agent who dealt with her requirements. Inside the shop, the yellowing walls were complimented by a sun-bleached computer, as the man took tentative sips from a chipped Mr Happy mug. They waited in silence for the computer to talk to the printer. Sheets of paper suddenly left the machine, which he stapled together and placed inside a large folder. It seemed more substantial for her twelve hundred pounds in cash.

That night she packed her bags, confident that a container ship wouldn't have stupid baggage limits. She had cleaned Victor inside and out and extended the insurance to cover Rosemary for a year. It still had the Jimmy Cliff tape in it when she parked outside the house. She dropped the keys through the letter box and scribbled a note.

'You can have Victor. But no more funerals. I'm off to catch a marlin. Love and kisses, Jill.'

The taxi drew up, they transferred her bags and headed for the docks. She'd never been on a ship before, nestled in her tiny cabin surrounded by thousands of containers filling the holds and deck. They pulled out of the mouth of the river and she saw her town from the sea for the first time, a thin line tracing her past. Jill watched it get fainter and fainter.

Scalp

A spot of red runs into the white snow, my blood staining the drift. I'm foamed up like Father Christmas, razor ready, staring into the mirror. Bald as a coot except for the sideboards, and I have to get them cut so they don't stick out, and make me stick out, like a sore thumb.

Brenda's voice snakes up the stairs, and under the door, 'Are you coming?'

She knows I'm in the bathroom, getting some peace the only way I know, except for the shed but it's too cold for that. Occasionally, I escape to the bog downstairs to read the football in the paper.

She knows I'm nowhere near ready, but it's the first warning in case I relax and enjoy myself. I know she loves me, she just wants to control me like a bull terrier on a short lead. I look closer, how can so little blood go so far? It's stopped bleeding now.

It doesn't make sense – it's the only hair I have got, and I spend ten minutes every day shaving it off. I'm tempted, why not? Grow a beard, let my hair down. They all had them in the old days. In the family album you can't see what they really look like, just rows of beards posing.

'Mostly chinless wonders,' Dad said, 'on your mother's side.' But he never really knew them, like I never knew him.

'Are you bloody coming?' I can hear *Eastenders* in the background as she leans into the hall, letting as little heat out of her snug as possible. The door slams. Three more warnings till the red alert.

He's twenty-one today. It doesn't seem possible. I can still feel a wet neck from his dribble, hear him singing in his bedroom, like tuning in to your favourite radio station.

He's a man now. That's me stuffed then.

We used to wash him in a little plastic bowl, cradle him in a towel and sprinkle him with talc, and then I'd blow a raspberry on his tummy, soft as silk. He'd gurgle. I had hair then. I'd tickle him with it, shaking my head from side to side, and sure as eggs he'd make a fountain of gratitude, so we had to dry him all over again.

He's six foot four now. I don't know if he gets oxygen up there. I'm five four myself; must have been a lofty milkman. He's bloody clever, good with numbers, something in the bank – money I hope. Gorgeous, curly blonde hair he's got, girls falling like flies, but he can't see it. It's wasted on a young head.

I pull the razor into the foam, like a snowplough, immaculate, a ritual. A slow tour of my face gradually reveals the ugly bastard to the world. Hello Harry, no change there then. This is the bit I like, the soft towel against the newly mown face, and the slap and sparkle of the aftershave. I'm glowing.

Paul used to spend hours in the bathroom, trying this hairstyle, then that one, followed by a selection of gels.

No gels in my day, just long hair, an expression of freedom. My old man would whistle at me in the street. When I asked him for pocket money he said, 'You know the deal son – no haircut, no money.' He really hacked me off. He bought us Jubilee crowns in nice little boxes, gleaming silver coins. I crept in one day and sneaked mine out of his top drawer. That would go towards a ticket to see Eric Clapton – when he was God.

Dad came home from the pub and looked pale, he told my mum the story the bank manager had told him. 'Youth today, God help us. One came in with a Jubilee crown. "We can't cash this," he told him. "It's not legal tender. I tell you what though; I'll buy it from you." He gave him five bob, dozy prat. He looked like a gypo, long curly hair, must have needed the cash badly.'

Dad eventually went to his drawer to confirm the worst. He never asked for it back. Besides, it was mine, and he never told me to get my hair cut again.

Sometimes when I look in the mirror, I don't know which face I'm looking at, the one that's there or the ones before with the frizz or the mullet.

I hate this bit, nasal hair. Brenda's like a hawk, she can spot one a mile off. Mirrors are unforgiving, you can see why they turn them to the wall when people pass away. We lost a baby after Paul. Bren didn't want any more after that. Can't blame her. It gave Paul more room in the back of the car, but I always thought we were like a three-legged table, vulnerable, easy to tip over. If we ever lost him, we'd be finished. I got Oscar, a bit of an insurance policy, a long-haired Jack Russell and a bloody good guard dog.

'We'll be late. Harry?' *Eastenders* has finished then.

I roll some deodorant on and then slip into my suit. I don't look too bad. Brenda's looked after herself, all that aerobic nonsense. Least I can do is say no to the extra pint, and walk past the snack machine. We don't make a bad couple really. Working in social services has given Bren a bit of an attitude, but get past that and she'd follow you down a sewer. Loyalty, what more could you ask for?

I've taken to wearing a hat lately. I read about the amount of body heat you lose through the top of your head, and how it's not good in the winter. Brenda must lose kilowatts through her mouth, but she says that's healthy exercise.

I've always fancied a trilby; I've hidden it in the wardrobe. I used to hide in there when I was a kid, so he wouldn't find me and give me the stick. I never hit Paul, not once. It's uncivilised, vulgar.

I place the hat on my head slowly, and add a little tilt, not too much. It's a nice brown one, top of the range, cost a few bob.

I grab another glimpse of the Adonis in the mirror and make my way downstairs. She's watching some reality TV programme where they get people to humiliate themselves for a bit of cash; no change there then.

'You're not going to wear that, are you?' I look at her as if she's stupid, then she's on the mickey take, doing tic-tac signs. 'I'll have a tenner each way on number six, and a fiver on the bloke in the hat to get sentimental over the brandies.'

'Sod off,' I mumble. I get the car keys, and watch her delay the departure for another five minutes, though she's been screaming at me to get ready for hours. Eventually we're going through the door together.

'You look nice Harry.' She plucks an imaginary hair from my shoulder. I wince, then give her a peck on the cheek.

Luigi's there to welcome us, he gives Bren a big kiss and me a weak handshake. We fitted his restaurant out last month and he's given us his Croydon one to do as well. He's as straight as a die, for a gay. He's got that little bit of hair combed over, a desperate act, but better than a syrup.

He shows us to a nice table near the back, with a bottle of Buck's Fizz on the house. Bren looks great in her new black number, but I think she might be having one of her hot flushes. I don't say anything, and pour her some water. Luigi takes her away to show her his holiday photos from Greece. I sit back and listen to Frank singing 'Chicago' and watch the other punters. The boy's late, but Bren returns, full of the Acropolis and the island she can't pronounce the name of.

'Why don't we go there, Harry? It looks lovely.' She looks round the room, a bit nervous. 'You can't leave your hat there. Put it with the coats.'

'You don't know how much I paid for it, love. There's only three of us, it'll be fine on the chair.'

Just then Luigi brings the birthday boy through. I'm speechless, my mouth open. I want to say something but nothing comes out.

'You look lovely darling, happy birthday,' Bren gives him a cuddle. He moves towards me. I get up, hold him, and mumble hopelessly. I want to rush to the barber's and gather his hair from the floor, put it with his first locks in the album.

'He's a chip off the old block, Harry. Looks nice doesn't it?' I rub the top of his head – as soft as a baby's bum. A tear runs down my cheek, I wipe it with my sleeve, sit down and look up at him. Bren reaches over and puts her hand on mine. A moment passes, I fumble.

'Twenty-one, you great streak. You're on your own now son.'

He laughs and gives me a soft punch on the shoulder. He slips past me. I watch him as love gushes from me, and he flops down in the chair, fifteen stone straight on my trilby.

'Sorry I'm late Mum, I've had a hard day.' He tries to get comfortable, and pulls it out from under him laughing at its flatness, crushed felt like a prop from Laurel and Hardy.

'Someone's going to be cheesed off,' he says, throwing it onto the other chair. He leans towards his mum. 'So, how's the grumpy bastard been then?'

Nothing Serious

The old man parts the grass with his walking stick, hoping there might be some clue to the boy's whereabouts. He only left his grandson for a few moments when he went round the back of the beach hut, but it took longer than he would have liked. His bladder refused to drain those last drops with any efficiency. They'd been playing peepo, the old man pretending he couldn't see, hiding his face behind cupped hands. Now the boy is out there somewhere playing by his own rules.

The old man has whittled the stick over the years until it feels like a part of him prodding the dune sand. He stops and takes in the sky as if he has forgotten his purpose again. He is back in the studio at the bottom of their garden, hidden under the rhododendrons, placing his father's face on the scanner, with a Chambers dictionary to weigh it down and ensure good contact. He wanted to catch every detail. It would be more than a replica. His father's magnified eye peered back at him from the computer screen, black pupil of hidden void; he'd never been so close to him. That's a lie. He used to roll across the carpet with him when he was a toddler, giggling as he smelt the sweet aftershave, praying it wouldn't finish and that he wouldn't wet himself. His father would hold him in the air, high above like an aeroplane, before the soft landing on the runway of his belly and the crash into the rough sandpaper chin. That face stared out at him in high resolution behind glass with pine frame, custodian of the stairwell. It would have been unfair to make his father watch them eat, or crap and piss. The stairs were a good compromise, a nod to his father each night as he went up to bed, with the occasional touch to realign the frame.

Something glimmers in the seagrass, a button, but it's too decorative for the boy. The old man has given up calling now, and goes through the order of the morning again.

'Can I go down to the beach, Grandpa?'

'Yes, as long as you stay in sight.'

The boy ran through the dunes, over the hill and out of view.

The wind gets stronger and the old man returns to the beach hut for a sweater, though he knows he should keep looking. Sitting in the old director's chair, he watches the paraffin burner warm the kettle and he tries to form a plan, but his mind drifts to his wife at the hospital.

Faith would be going through the tunnel now, flat on her back, hemmed in, no good for claustrophobics. She'd be dressed in a hospital smock, with stains that they couldn't wash away. But would they find other stains, deep inside?

She wouldn't let him go with her, and took Sue their daughter instead. The radiotherapist would have left her alone by now, with the soft drone and flashing lights. They'd send her down that white tunnel to be scanned like a can of peas at the supermarket. He wished he'd gone but she'd resisted.

He spilt the tea as he emptied the kettle into the chipped enamel mug. The wind blew up and a broken kite flew across the path in front of the huts. He shuddered and carried the mug through the dunes, down to the sea. He called as loud as he could, but the wind stole the child's name and threw it out to sea. His eyes were failing him, the salt and sand made his body stiffen as he struggled on towards the water. The tide was coming in, wiping footprints. He found nothing and clambered back up the paths between the beach huts calling the boy's name. Paedophiles had crossed his mind, but he hated the popular press scaremongering. Now, he was seeing headlines and that photo filling TV screens and posters, the one he took at Christmas. A course of anger hit him, he swore at the boy under his breath and wanted to punish him, but the moment passed. If he could have pissed quicker he might have seen where the boy went. From above the rocks and the beach huts, he saw Faith and Sue driving into the car park.

He watched them get out of the car, and tried to read their body language, as they walked up the path. What in the world would he say to them about the boy? He could feel his father's eye leering at him, and a cold sweat ran down his neck. The path twisted down between the cliffs and he hurried back towards the hut biting his lip.

'Peepo.' The boy leapt out from behind the hut. The old man turned and grabbed him. He kissed his neck and threw him round and round in a dance of celebration, rubbing his stubble against the boy's soft face.

'Don't Grandpa, you're too rough.'

He put the boy down and wiped back the tears from his face.

Faith touched the old man lightly on his cheek and stood with a soft smile on her face. He collapsed in a chair cradling the boy in his lap.

'Well?' he raised an inquisitive eyebrow.

'Nothing serious. Just a silly scare.' Faith busied herself filling the kettle. She bent down to look at the boy. 'So, what have you been up to?'

'We've been playing peepo, haven't we Grandpa?'

The old man nodded and squeezed the boy until he shrieked.

Wishbone Duty

Mansell took the back roads. The rifle on the passenger seat would be a distraction, should he meet anyone. He didn't want small talk or patronising words from neighbours who were scarce when his Elsie was drifting. If he had to stop, they would think he was going hunting, but in truth he was doing the opposite. Pickle lay in the back chewing the bone.

Dusk was falling as the headlights of the Land Rover shone a sepia path through the flatlands. Mansell could see his breath as he changed gear to cross the River Bly and then opened her up on the plateau heading west. The beam lit the deep brown earth that would yield the lion's share of next year's wheat harvest. He had ploughed those fields in his youth for Ezra Frost, but they were all contract farms now. The jeep droned for another ten miles and he stared at the theatrical backdrop that never moved or got any closer. The engine's vibration was hypnotic and he shivered as wind blew through the hole where the heater used to be. Pickle climbed onto the front seat to get some of Mansell's warmth, but he pushed the dog onto the floor. After the plateau they clung to rolling hills through black woods till the road opened towards the remote villages where tourists lost more than their hubcaps. Elsie was born here and met Mansell on the fields. He hadn't been back for years, but he knew the land as good as his palm. Pickle came from her village, the runt of the litter. The dog tried again, clawing the torn upholstery, but was slapped down as Mansell cursed his persistence. He was Elsie's dog, a pest. Mansell would have preferred a cat or a loft full of pigeons.

A strong wind blew as they crossed more plains, like a shadow puppet on a long stage beneath the darkening sky. The road began to sparkle and the jeep left tracks in the frost as it skidded and turned down the track, coming to a halt. The headlights shone across the gravel and into the slope of a deep quarry. Pickle followed him down to the edge. Crows cawed and circled the trees as the wind picked up. Mansell leant against the jeep, warming himself on the bonnet, and lit a cigarette as the engine ticked over. Pickle fetched his ball from the back seat, Mansell kicked it away and the dog retrieved it. This was repeated several times, until he threw the half-smoked cigarette to the ground. The dog followed his muddied boots to the quarry's edge and sleet began to fall. Mansell clenched his teeth, pulled his arm back and threw the ball as far as he had ever wanted to throw anything. Pickle took to the chase tumbling into the void. Backing the jeep up, Mansell pushed his foot to the floor and roared into the night. The journey home would be quicker, where he could sit in front of the fire and read his steam train magazine. His life would be simpler without her dog.

A desk calendar showed a red 24 on the polished oak desk, next to the brass plaque, 'Sarah Pargeter – Family Mediation Officer'. After brushing her teeth in the partners' restroom Sarah squeezed the wash bag into her new leather holdall and cursed, as she had planned to leave earlier but for the arbitration meeting. It was about a misunderstanding over child custody arrangements. She had observed the two ex-lovers struggle to find ways of being angry with dignity.

As her new Toyota Prius followed the motorway north she relaxed and savoured the long journey watching the city drop away, proud in the knowledge that her car was not harming the environment. Damage limitation was an important part of Sarah's life, preferable to the vagaries of love. She tuned in to a radio station where DJs offered platitudes to relatives trying to get home for the holiday weekend.

Pulling in to the services, she parked next to a couple with children.

'Are you sure we don't need any milk?' the man asked his wife, pulling himself out of the car.

'God knows,' she replied, 'but you'd better get some, and a bunch of flowers if they're any good.' He stretched his arms up to the sky, as one of the children ran after him. Sarah watched from a distance then followed them past the Salvation Army band into the shop, where she bought some food, praline chocolates and Turkish Delight, his favourite. After dropping some change into the bandsman's bucket she tapped Mansell's number into her Blackberry, and took some deep breaths before she got back into the car.

'Dad it's me. I'm a bit behind, I'm afraid.' She teased her hair in the mirror. 'No, not too bad. ETA?' She raised her eyes. 'About eightish. No, a sandwich would be fine.' ETA came from his train days, a guard on the east coast line. Work on the land had dried up, but he had enjoyed the toing and froing across the fens, while Sarah got a train south to the convent school where she had won a scholarship.

Mansell got the old hoover out, held together with tape and string, and ran it across the worn carpet, then tidied his train books. He scraped the last of Pickle's food into the bin and hid the bowls in the outhouse.

Sarah's headlights lit up the old cottage with the smoking chimney as she swerved into the drive. Sitting still in the car, she killed the lights and prepared herself. She'd made it, another year being a solicitor in suburbia, three dinner dates but no follow-ups, a holiday in Greece with Martin, all walking and talking. She looked at the garden, her childhood hiding place behind the shed. What happened to that little girl and all she was going to achieve? Smoke blew east from the chimney, as if the cottage was leaving its harbour. Now Sarah was here she wasn't sure she could do it again. The déjà vu welled up inside her. She grabbed a bottle of wine from the boot and locked the car. It was colder than down south, the apple tree reached out over the bonnet, desperate for pruning. She ducked under a branch and walked up the path, as his silhouette greeted her. They hugged; it was easier in the dark. He smelt of tobacco and old age, she of Chanel No.5 and anxious sweat.

'Good journey?' Mansell asked.

'Okay. Bit of a crisis at work.'

'I'll put the kettle on.' He let her go into the cottage first. It was just the same except the colours had faded, bathed in a soft yellow. He pulled the curtains so no one would see them and to lessen the draughts.

'Where's Pickle?' Sarah asked.

'I had to take him to the vet.' He got some mugs from the cupboard. 'Nasty business, but it was for the best.'

'You didn't tell me.'

'There's nothing you could do. Earl Grey?'

'Yes, please.'

'Good, I got some in specially.'

Sarah went into the sitting room, sat on the sofa and looked at the space where Pickle might have been. 'Was he in pain?' She patted the cushion but no dog jumped up, so she couldn't stroke or pat him.

Mansell carried the tea in with some sandwiches. 'The vet was marvellous, put him to sleep. It was peaceful.' He passed the mug over and smiled.

'It must have been awful for you.' She cradled the drink and looked round the room. The mantelpiece with pictures of her at school and graduating, the carriage clock, an old clay pipe he dug up. The amateur painting of the fens, a snow scene with a church nestling behind a hill. On the sideboard there was a picture of their wedding, and Sarah thought of her mother obscured by a new misty veil.

'How's Mum?'

He lit his pipe. 'Hard to say, she's in her own world. I took her some flowers.'

'That's nice.'

'Thanks for the cheque. I paid the home.'

He got up and went to the sideboard.

'Did she recognise you?'

He didn't answer, but passed a card over. 'Bill and Mandy have had a little boy.'

She couldn't remember when she'd last seen her cousin, probably the wedding.

'New rug?' she asked.

'Bloody fire caught the carpet.'

'Nice colour.'

'Boot fair, Elmsfield, three quid.'

The *Radio Times* was on the drinks table by his armchair, hiding the coasters from Cromer Pier.

'Morecambe and Wise are on at ten, it's a repeat.'

'Better the devil you know.' She sipped her tea and smiled at him. She knew it was best to be a child, cosy by the fire. They watched the television, ate chocolates and picked at conversation. Sarah looked at his frayed cardigan; he was made of memories unravelling. He looked at her short hair, where long curls used to hang. Business had made her more like a man, always busy, her Blackberry loaded with meetings and contingency plans.

Sarah went outside and got her things from the car and took them up to her old bedroom. It was frozen in time. She put a hot water bottle in the bed and switched the electric fire on. Mansell's laughter drifted up the stairs, quavering on the edge. She used the ground-floor bathroom and apologised for her tiredness. With thick socks on, she got into bed and pulled the blankets round her just as the clock struck midnight. She sighed and put her wristwatch on the bedside table and switched out the light.

In the morning Mansell stoked the fire and they drank tea in their dressing gowns. She gave him the large box wrapped in metallic paper. His big hands untied the ribbons and folded the paper up before he pulled the present out of the box. He looked at her with love and curiosity.

'It's a laptop, Dad.'

He held it away from him as if it might explode.

'I've organised broadband for you. A man'll come and fit it. Then we'll be able to email.'

'How much is all that?'

'Twenty-four ninety-nine a month. Don't worry, I'm doing all right.'

He put the laptop aside. 'I've looked at the world-wide-web in the library. Couldn't get on with it.' Throwing another log on the fire he sat back in his chair. 'You shouldn't have done it. It's too much.'

'Don't be silly, it's nothing.' Sarah pulled her dressing gown over her knees to keep warm. Mansell passed her a small package. He'd bought her an amaryllis wrapped in an old magazine. She kissed him on the cheek but his stubble irritated her.

After a shower she got the food from the car and prepared the roast. She took the vegetable peelings to the compost, and walked round the garden. He appeared behind her.

'Did you bury Pickle?'

'No, the vet sorted everything.' He turned away. 'I'm getting the ashes next week.' They looked out over the fields and a sharp wind blew between them.

'I'd better put the spuds in.' Sarah strolled back inside.

As usual the hours of preparation were erased by the minutes of consumption, but at least she got the wishbone. She reached across the table, her little finger clasping the bone, he attached his and they pulled. Sarah wished for the future and a different Christmas in another country. Mansell wished for the past, a slower world, dancing with Elsie in the village hall. The bone snapped and they pulled their hands apart. Sarah smiled, skiing somewhere in the Alps with an admirer.

She washed the dishes as the Queen's speech with perfect diction mesmerised a tired Mansell into sleep. Her

Majesty was a landmark, a constant in this sea of change. His eyes closed and Sarah went for a walk down the lanes.

She'd baked the cake herself, icing and marzipan that she had never liked, insulating the fruit. It was tradition. She left the white snow and yellow layer on the side of her plate.

'Don't you want it?' Mansell pointed. She shook her head, savouring the fruit.

'Waste not want not.' He filled his mouth.

'I might go and visit Mum,' she said without thinking.

'It's up to you, but there's not much point.'

It was for herself that she wanted to go, but maybe there was no point if the person she wanted to see wasn't there.

'Could I have some of the ashes?'

Mansell froze with cake in mid-air and mouth open.

'Sorry,' he furrowed his brow.

'Pickle, Pickle's ashes, could you mail me some?'

He leant back, with his hands against the edge of the table.

'For closure. I'd like that.'

'Do they allow that? Ashes through the post?' Mansell put the cake in his mouth.

'They wouldn't know would they?'

He shook his head and kept eating.

Sarah left the table and decided to clean the bathroom. She locked the door and sat on the edge of the bath with her Blackberry. There were no messages. She tapped the keys and sent a text to Martin, she might drop by tomorrow to give him his present. She wiped the bath and ran the hot tap. As she went upstairs to fetch a towel, Mansell was watching a film about the Flying Scotsman. There were two candles under the sink, she lit them and put them on saucers. Immersing herself in the steaming hot water, she watched the candles gutter in the draught.

Mansell switched the film off, put the laptop back in its box and took Sarah's car keys from her bag. He crept through the back door and lit the path with his torch. Unlocking the boot of her car, he hid the laptop under the travelling rug. An owl flew across the cottage towards the neighbouring farm as he closed the boot. Sarah was humming to herself in the bath, when he made his way up to bed.

She woke at seven to hear his snoring down the hall. The room seemed smaller than ever, with condensation on the cracked Crittall window that she had escaped through when she ran away south, when she thought she was grown up and used make-up for the first time. That was exactly how she felt now, the very same person with a map too small for all the places she knew the names of, but a map too large to feel part of. It's much quicker packing for a return journey; she didn't bother to fold her clothes. Composing a note in her head she crept downstairs, and carried her bags out to the car. She needed the loo and would leave a note in the kitchen, but when she came out of the bathroom he was standing there forlorn in his dressing gown. She wanted to push him away but he turned and went to the window.

'There's a snow flurry.' He watched a sprinkling of white cover the garden muting the colours. 'Could get nasty.'

'The forecast isn't very good.' Sarah filled a glass with orange juice and swallowed quickly.

'You should take some of that stuff with you. I won't eat it.'

'Don't be ridiculous.'

He stoked the fire. 'I never asked you about your work.'

'It's crazy. Got a text last night, someone needs me. It never stops.'

He nodded and threw some kindling onto the red embers. 'No one is indispensable.'

She turned the pages of a local paper, advertising Boxing Day sales, with promises of free credit. She closed it and got her handbag.

'Sorry I've got to dash.'

'Probably best with the weather.' He pulled his duffle coat on, over his dressing gown.

'Don't come out Dad.'

He ignored her and pushed his feet into the old boots. By the car, she gave him a kiss and he stood still, rooted. She wound the window down. 'Good luck with the laptop, I'll email you.'

Mansell watched the smoke from the exhaust draw a line as she pulled away down the lane, waving out of the window. He turned slowly back onto the path, tracing steps as he trod on her crisp footprints.

A familiar shape came bounding across the garden. As it

got nearer it barked and jumped up at him wagging its tail. He shook his head and kept walking. The dog was filthy with some blood on its neck. Mansell held the door open and let Pickle in. 'I'll put you on a bloody plane next time.' Shutting the door he noticed her amaryllis on the kitchen table and placed it on a saucer by the window.

Dave Pescod was born in London. His stories have been broadcast on BBC Radio 4 and published in *Dreamcatcher, Transmission*, Route Anthologies, on the British Commonwealth Short Story Competition CD 2009, in the *Grist Anthology 2011* and the *Bridport Prize Anthology 2011*. He lives in Cambridge.

Acknowledgements
I would like to thank my wife Kate, Ian Daley, Digby Beaumont, The 134 Club, Susan Williams, Michelle Spring, Rukhsana Ahmad, Katharine McMahon, my three sons and Andy Love for all their encouragement, support and honesty which made this book possible.

For further information on this book,
and for Route's full book programme
please visit:

www.route-online.com

Lightning Source UK Ltd.
Milton Keynes UK
UKOW04f0731300815

257758UK00002BA/18/P

9 781907 862076